GUNS + TACOS

Season Three, Volume 5

GUNS + TACOS

Season One
Tacos de Cazuela con Smith & Wesson by Gary Phillips
Three Brisket Tacos and a Sig Sauer by Michael Bracken
A Gyro and a Glock by Frank Zafiro
Three Chalupas, Rice, Soda...and a Kimber .45
by Trey R. Barker
Some Churros and El Burro by William Dylan Powell
A Beretta, Burritos, and Bears by James A. Hearn

Season Two
Burritos & Bullets by Eric Beetner
Jalapeño Poppers and a Flare Gun
by Michael Bracken & Trey R. Barker
Four Shrimp Tacos and a Walther P38 by Alec Cizak
Taco, a T-Bird, a Beretta and One Furious Night
by Ann Aptaker
Sopa and a Streetsweeper by Ryan Sayles
Dos Tacos Guatemaltecos y Una Pistola Casera
by Mark Troy

Season Three
Two More Tacos, a Beretta .32,
and a Pink Butterfly by Dave Zeltserman
Two Tamales, One Tokarev,
and a Lifetime of Broken Promises by Stacy Woodson
Chimichangas and a Couple of Glocks
by David H. Hendrickson
Refried Beans and a Snub-Nosed .44 by Hugh Lessig
Two Steak Taco Combos and a Pair of Sig Sauers
by Neil S. Plakcy
A Smith & Wesson with a Side of Chorizo
by Andrew Welsh-Huggins

DAVE ZELTSERMAN,
STACY WOODSON,
AND DAVID H. HENDRICKSON

GUNS + TACOS

Season Three, Volume 5

SERIES CREATED AND EDITED BY
MICHAEL BRACKEN & TREY R. BARKER

Down & Out Books
3959 Van Dyke Road, Suite 265
Lutz, FL 33558
DownAndOutBooks.com

Cover design by Zach McCain

ISBN: 1-64396-259-0
ISBN-13: 978-1-64396-259-7

CONTENTS

There's a taco truck in Chicago known among a certain segment of the population for its daily specials. Late at night and during the wee hours of the morning, it isn't the food selection that attracts customers, it's the illegal weapons available with the special order. Each episode of *Guns + Tacos* features the story of one Chicagoland resident who visits the taco truck seeking a solution to life's problems, a solution that always comes in a to-go bag.

GUNS+TACOS CREATED AND EDITED BY   MICHAEL BRACKEN & TREY R. BARKER

DAVE ZELTSERMAN

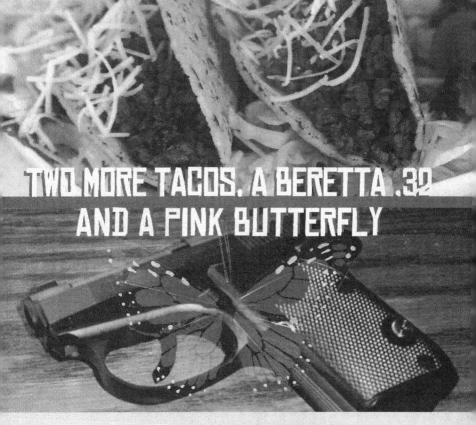

TWO MORE TACOS, A BERETTA .32 AND A PINK BUTTERFLY

SEASON **3**

EPISODE **13**

OTHER TITLES BY DAVE ZELTSERMAN

TWO MORE TACOS, A BERETTA .32, AND A PINK BUTTERFLY

Dave Zeltserman

To Chicago writer, Michael Black,
who knows the dark side of the street.

Part One: Danny Meadows

Danny Meadows plodded down the five stone steps leading to the basement-level Kinzie Street bar. The day had been brighter than normal for September, and after stepping inside the aptly named Broken Drum, Meadows stood for a moment to give his eyes a chance to adjust to the darkness of the place. It had been two months since his last visit, and it still had the same tin ceiling and dark wood paneling. Although the owner poured sixty thousand dollars into remodeling the place and upgrading the kitchen, it still looked like a dive. *Wasted money*, Meadows thought, not that he cared. The fact that the bar was nearly empty proved his point.

3

The bartender was new. At least he hadn't seen her before. Early thirties, maybe. A redhead. A little too pale and ten pounds too skinny. Still, he liked seeing the tightness that showed around her mouth when she forced a smile in his direction. He also enjoyed seeing the fear glistening in her very large eyes as she watched him approach the shiny, new brass bar that she stood behind; one of a number of useless improvements the owner had made. Meadows couldn't blame her for the way she reacted to him. He was a large, hulking man with a scary toughness about him, but there was more to it than that. Once someone got a good enough look at his eyes and mouth, they quickly understood his true nature. Cruelty. He had business that afternoon, but if he had time later he would have fun with her. He took a seat on a new red leather barstool and smiled inwardly as he caught the hitch alongside her mouth that momentarily wrecked her smile.

Meadows peered past her so he could study the bottles lining the back shelf. The owner had upgraded his booze, not that it had done any good in making the place profitable. He shifted his gaze back to the bartender and told her which bourbon he wanted, and told her to bring over the bottle and a glass with a couple of ice cubes.

"I can't do that," she said.

"Sure you can, darling." He showed her an open-mouthed smile that would've looked right at home on a rattlesnake. "Joe's in his office, right? Give him a call and tell him Danny Meadows is here. He'll tell you it's okay."

The way his eyes deadened convinced her to leave him the bottle and a glass. He poured himself a double and took his time sipping it. The bartender moved to the end of the bar and fidgeted as she cut up a plate of limes, but she couldn't get out from under his gaze. Soon she was wilting under it.

Yeah, he was going to have fun with her later.

"Be seeing you, darling," Meadows said. He pushed himself off the barstool, grabbed the bottle and glass, and headed to an office in the back where he found the owner, Joe Harney,

4

scowling at a stack of bills. Meadows wore crepe-soled shoes and could be quiet when he wanted to be, and Harney didn't notice as he pulled up a chair. It wasn't until Meadows put his size thirteen feet on the desk that Harney looked up. He blinked twice before he seemed to recognize Meadows. His shoulders slumped then, but he tried to bluff him as he maintained his gruff exterior and told Meadows that he was surprised to see him.

"You shouldn't be."

"What are you talking about? I told your man only three days ago I'll have the money next Monday."

Meadows opened his eyes wide in mock surprise. "The whole ninety-three grand?" he asked, because that was how much Harney's sixty grand loan had swelled to, even though Harney had made most of his payments on time.

"Ninety-three grand? Are you nuts? Of course not, only what I owe for the past two weeks." He made a face as if he had swallowed something unpleasant tasting. "Plus the added interest."

Meadows didn't like anyone implying that he was crazy, and he was tempted to smash in Harney's fat face with the bourbon bottle, but Raskins had told him that his uncle wanted this done quietly, if possible, so instead he took his time pouring himself another double shot of bourbon. After drinking down most of it, he swung his feet off the desk, and leaned forward, his face hardening into something violent.

"It don't work that way," he said. "You're late. That means you either pay up what you owe now or you sign this paper."

Meadows put down the glass so he could slip a folded contract from his inside jacket pocket and hand it to Harney. The bar owner's face fell flat as he read what he was given.

"You can't be serious," he said, his bluster from earlier gone, and his voice now a tinny whisper. "Until last week I never missed a payment. Not once. One mistake and you're going to take my place from me?"

"You could've been working the bar instead of hiring a piece of ass. If you had, maybe you would've had the money for us on time, but you wanted a little action on the side."

Harney's face flushed with anger. "That's my niece, you bastard. She's helping me out of the goodness of her heart."

"Watch your mouth," Meadows warned.

"You goddamn jackals," Harney swore. "I've already paid back forty grand and you're going to take my bar because I'm late once?"

"I told you to watch your mouth." Meadows picked his glass up from the floor and took his time draining the rest of its contents. All the while Harney grew increasingly agitated to the point where it looked like he had trouble staying seated. "We're going to take better care of you than you deserve. We'll let you stay on to run the bar. And we'll pay you a salary that's going to be better than what you're taking home now."

"Conaway need a front, is that it? What's he going to use my place for? Running drugs? Whores? Bookmaking?"

Meadows dropped his glass to the terracotta tiled floor, letting it shatter. He took a stiletto switchblade from his pants pocket and released its five-inch blade.

"I'll tell you what. You ever stick your nose into my boss's business again, and I'll slice it off."

Harney stared transfixed at the blade before forcing himself to look back into Meadows's eyes. He cleared his throat and tried to glower at Meadows, but it was a halfhearted attempt.

"What if I refuse to sign?" he asked with a laughably false bravado.

"One of the following happens then: I either cut off your hand and sign the contract for you, or I cut you to pieces and then offer the sap who inherits this place from you the same deal." A nastiness glinted in Meadows's eyes. "Or maybe I have myself some real fun and I drag your niece in here and slice off pieces of her until you sign."

Meadows's cell phone rang, interrupting him just as he was beginning to enjoy himself. He planted his switchblade into the surface of the wooden desk, grabbed the phone, and glared at it to see that Raskins was calling. He wanted to ignore the call, but he couldn't ignore the "Toad." Annoyed, he turned away from Harney and answered the phone, telling Raskins that he was busy.

"Your uncle says otherwise. I need to see you."

His uncle was Charlie Conaway. The big boss. "Can you give me an hour?"

"No. This is important. Get your ass in here."

Raskins ended the call from his end. Meadows jaw clenched, forcing his mouth into what might've been mistaken at first glance as a smile. He turned back to Harney and ordered him to sign the damn paper. The soon-to-be former owner of the Broken Drum did as he was told.

Meadows was in a sour mood when he walked up to Jesse's Taco truck. The urgent matter Raskins wanted to see him about wasn't all that urgent—at least nothing that required Meadows to drop everything and rush over for a meeting. Instead, it was only because his uncle was pissed and Raskins was trying to placate the old man. One of his uncle's bagmen, a jerkoff by the name of Trevor Haywood, had been ripping him off, and his uncle wanted blood. Okay. Meadows understood that. But the meeting could've happened an hour later. It could've happened two or even three hours later for that matter.

Because of that, Meadows was itching for a fight, but when he saw that the heifer-sized broad named Jessie was working the truck, he knew he wouldn't be getting one from her. The dame had been on the job the first time Meadows made use of their service to get himself a cheap, untraceable, throwaway gun, and he was too amused by the setup to bother telling her that he worked for Big Charlie Conaway. Because of that, when she handed him his "special of the day" package with a pair of greasy pork tacos inside and a toy cap gun, things went sideways fast.

He naturally complained about what he was given, and instead of trying to rectify the situation, Jessie grabbed a sawed-off shotgun from beneath the counter with the intention of pointing it at him, maybe even taking off his head. Well, she might've weighed two and a half bills and looked meaner than any South Side alley rat, but that didn't stop Meadows from snatching the shotgun away from her and bouncing her around a bit. He also made her uglier than she already had been, which was quite a feat since a cord of ugly sticks must've already been used on her. By the time he was done, her nose was flatter than any of their tacos, and he had chiseled a half dozen more scars out of her granite block of a face.

Meadows flashed a nasty grin. "As usual, a sight for sore eyes."

Jessie stood like a stone block behind the counter, her face showing nothing. Her lips moving just slightly more than a ventriloquist's, she answered back, "As usual, as charming as a bag of lice."

Meadows had to laugh. Just like that, his bad mood was gone. Without waiting for Meadows to say anything, Jessie took out one of their special bags, looked inside, then grabbed another bag and did the same. Meadows paid her and took the second bag from her. Inside were two tacos wrapped in aluminum foil and a Beretta thirty-two caliber.

"What was in the first bag?"

Jessie's poker face cracked. "A starter pistol."

Meadows shook his head, dumbfounded by this. "Why the fuck would you try to stick someone with that?"

"It's the luck of the draw."

"I'm amazed you haven't been popped yet," Meadows said. "I truly am."

Jessie swallowed back whatever crack had popped into her head, and her eyes glazed. It was obvious to Meadows that as far as she was concerned they were done. He told her that he'd be seeing her again when the need arose. He tossed the tacos and waited until he was alone in his car before checking out the Beretta. The gun had seen better days and needed a cleaning, but the magazine was fully loaded and it looked like it was in working order. He'd scrub the barrel later and rub in some gun oil, and maybe take a ride to LaBagh Woods to fire off a couple of rounds just to be sure. Or maybe he'd find an empty alley for target practice. He'd see how he felt later.

He headed back to his apartment to take care of the pistol. It was only a quarter past five, leaving him plenty of time to get all this done. He got on the phone and made reservations for nine at his favorite Italian restaurant, Scalia's. He might as well load up on carbs, since it would be much later after that before he'd be taking care of the business his uncle had given him, and he was going to have a long night ahead of him. He had little doubt that he'd be busy until morning, not that he minded.

The assignment waiting for him was the kind he enjoyed most. He was going to be taking his time with it.

Meadows waited until three in the morning before entering the South Wabash Avenue apartment building where Haywood had a ground-level apartment. The lock on Haywood's door wouldn't have been difficult to pick, but Meadows didn't need a lock pick to gain entrance since Raskins had provided him with a key.

The lights were off inside the apartment and the place was as quiet as a crypt. Meadows, who wore cloth gardening gloves and had on a dark ski mask and black clothing, was careful closing the front door, then stood still until his eyes adjusted better to the dark. He had brought along a gym bag that had everything he was going to need that night to make it as bloody as his uncle wanted it. In their line of work, messaging was important.

He flashed a penlight to locate the bedroom door and identify furniture that he would need to avoid. He took a zip tie from his jacket pocket and headed over to the closed bedroom door, hoping that he'd find Trevor Haywood inside.

Meadows again used his penlight after he opened the door to get a lay of the room. A smile twisted his lips when he heard someone snoring under the blanket. He walked quietly over to the bed and carefully removed the blanket to reveal that Haywood was alone and sleeping fitfully on his stomach. Meadows zip-tied Haywood's wrists together and flipped him onto his back. It took a minute of flashing the penlight into Haywood's eyes before he woke up.

"What the hell," Haywood murmured, his voice froggy.

Meadows shushed him. "Where's the money you stole from Conaway?" he asked.

Haywood was fully awake then, his eyes showing an alertness as he grasped his situation. "I don't know what you're talking about, buddy," he claimed in an aggrieved tone. "I didn't steal nothing."

Along with the zip ties, Meadows also had a pair of wool socks in his jacket pocket for easy access. He pinched Haywood's nostrils closed until his victim was forced to open his mouth to breathe, and then he shoved the socks into Haywood's mouth, gagging him.

"I'm going to hurt you now," Meadows said. "How much I hurt you is all up to you, sport."

Meadows wouldn't be able to use his trademark stiletto switchblade on Haywood without giving away who he was, so he took a four-inch hunting knife from his gym bag and used that to make deep cuts into Haywood's face. The bagman strained against his restraints and his eyes bulged as Meadows disfigured him, his frantic screaming muffled by the socks. After Meadows sliced up both of Haywood's cheeks, he pulled out the socks and asked him again where the money was, and this time Haywood told him.

Haywood had fitted a false panel in the back of his bedroom closet, and after Meadows removed it, he found a shopping bag filled with Charlie Conaway's money. He brought the bag with him as he first turned on the lights and then removed his ski mask. The point of wearing the ski mask earlier was so that Haywood would think he had a chance of living if he gave up the money. He knew who Meadows was, and for a few brief heartbeats fear shone in his eyes, but then they quickly dulled as resignation set in and he accepted what would be happening to him.

Meadows took his time and was as careful with his use of the blade as a sculptor might've been with a chisel and a block of Italian marble, which in a way made sense since he considered himself an artist and Trevor Haywood his canvas, and the medium he was working in was pain. He was so caught up in what he was doing that he didn't hear the rush of movement behind him. It was only when he heard the door latch for the bedroom clicking open that he turned around and saw the naked woman fleeing the room. She was on the short side, slender, and blond, but what caught his attention was the pink butterfly tattooed on her right butt cheek.

The door slammed shut behind her and it was only then that he broke out of his stupor. He ran to the door, but he couldn't open it. His gloves were too slick with blood and gore for him to get a firm enough grasp on the doorknob.

Godammit!

Meadows was still struggling to rip the glove from his right hand when he heard a window being opened, followed by the sound of someone climbing through it. While it might've only taken seconds, it seemed far longer for him to get the glove off and the door open. As he expected, a window in the living room had been opened. He moved over to it, stuck his head out, and saw that it opened onto an alley. The alley appeared empty, but the girl could've been hiding either behind a dumpster at one end of it or a cluster of garbage cans at the other end.

Goddammit!

He had a decision to make. He could either chase after her

now or potentially waste valuable time finishing up with Trevor Haywood. Seconds ticked by as he stood frozen, indecisive. He tried to remember whether she was carrying anything when she fled the room and had a vague recollection of a bundle of clothing in her arms. He squeezed his eyes closed and tried harder to remember, and was pretty sure that was the case. If it was, she must've also had her pocketbook in that bundle, which meant she'd have her phone. Which also meant she could be calling the police at any moment. Which further meant if he chased after her now and didn't find her, he might not have a chance to get back into the apartment so he could finish up with Haywood.

Goddammit!

He had to accept that he had no choice on the matter. He stripped off his remaining blood-soaked glove and headed back into the bedroom. Haywood was in rough shape with nearly a third of his skin sliced off, but he'd live if he were left as he was. Even if he wouldn't, Meadows had his orders. His uncle wanted a clip emptied out under Haywood's chin to leave a message as to who was behind Haywood's death and why. You rip off Big Charlie Conaway and this is what happens. Meadows rummaged through his gym bag, found his ear protectors, and slipped them on, along with a clean pair of gloves. He then used the gun he had gotten from Jesse's so he could leave his uncle's signature, along with most of Haywood's brains splattered on the wall behind the bed. That done, he dropped the gun onto the floor, put his ski mask back on, and grabbed his gym bag and the shopping bag holding his uncle's money. He was about to leave the bedroom when he spotted a pair of women's shoes that must've been left behind by the girl with the pink butterfly tattoo. He stuck the shoes in the gym bag, gave the room another quick look and decided that the girl must've heard him entering the apartment and hid under the bed. It was funny that she'd do that instead of waking Haywood and telling him that they had an intruder, but you could never figure out why people did the stuff they did, especially skirts.

He lifted the blanket enough to see that there would've been enough room for someone skinny, like that girl, to have squeezed under there. So she bided her time and waited for a chance to escape. Jesus, she must've gotten a good look at him. Forget about picking him out of a lineup, she'd be able to describe him in detail down to the mole next to his left eye.

Goddammit!

She had to be found. He wouldn't be able to sleep peacefully at night until she was. And if his uncle learned about this...

Goddammit!

He left the bedroom and continued through the apartment until he got to the front door. Once out of the apartment, he locked the door behind him since he wasn't in the habit making things any easier for the cops, and then made a beeline for the fire door in back. A thirty-two pistol wasn't exactly a peashooter—it made noise, but not enough to get any of Haywood's neighbors opening their doors. Once outside, Meadows made a hard right and walked briskly to the alley that Haywood's living room looked over. There was no girl, naked or otherwise, hiding behind or in the dumpster. For all the good it did him, he raced to the other end to see that she wasn't behind the garbage cans either. As far as he could tell, there was no sign that she'd ever been in the alley.

He considered calling Raskins and asking that little toad to send someone to lift fingerprints off the windowsill, but he just didn't feel up to telling Raskins about this fiasco yet since it would've been the same as telling his uncle. Besides, the cops could be at the apartment building any minute.

Goddammit!

Meadows had parked on East 67th, and the streets were empty as he walked to his car. He drove down South Michigan, South Hartwell, and South Indiana, and no sign of the girl. She could've been hiding behind any of the apartment buildings or in the backyards of the houses he drove past, or she could've already been in the wind. He thought about getting on foot and looking for her, but that just seemed like a fool's errand that could cause a concerned homeowner to call the police. He had to accept that he wasn't going to find her.

He drove back to South Wabash and parked half a block away from Haywood's building. Still no cops. If she were going to call the cops that night, she would've already done so, and they'd already be there. He sat for several minutes thinking the matter over and then left the car. This time instead of walking into the building and risking seeing one of Haywood's neighbors, he used the open window off of the alley. It was a tough squeeze getting his body through it, and at one point he was afraid he might've gotten stuck which would've been damn embarrassing, to say the least, but once he forced himself to relax and to quit struggling, he slipped through.

He gave the bedroom and living room a more thorough search trying to find anything that the girl might've left behind. He looked through a hallway closet for a woman's coat and the bathroom for medication prescribed to anyone other than Haywood. Nothing. If the girl had been a frequent visitor, she hadn't been frequent enough to leave anything like that behind.

Meadows left the way he came in.

Part Two: Lance

Detective Simon Weller checked his cell phone after the text message signal and saw the selfie that Captain Lou Marin had sent him.

"Food's here," he announced.

His partner, Mike Souza, was closer to the hotel room door, so he answered it while ignoring protocol and leaving his gun holstered. Captain Marin stood on the other side, looking annoyed that he had had to interrupt his evening to deliver food to his detectives. He handed a bag to Souza and warned his detective to keep the witness safe. "Grand jury tomorrow," he

14

said. "Be alert, okay."

Souza gave his captain a weary grin. After all, they were already on their fourth week babysitting Ned Wilson's former underling turned rat. This was their first night back in Madison, arriving that afternoon since they had to be in court at nine-thirty the next morning. Everything had gone smoothly in getting their witness into the hotel unseen.

"Nothing to worry about, Captain."

"Famous last words," Marin said. He stepped into the room, closed the door behind him so as not to make a sound other than the latch clicking shut, and pushed past Souza so he could take several steps into the hotel suite and give Detective Weller a hard eye. "Stay on your toes," he ordered. "No slip ups."

"Aye aye, Captain," Weller said with a smirk and a salute.

Marin mumbled something to himself about the clowns he had working for him, but left it at that. After he left the suite and Souza had locked the door behind him, Weller knocked on the bedroom door and announced that dinner had arrived.

Henry Lutcher walked out. Lutcher, a short balding heavyset man with a round, red face, was the very definition of the word *roly-poly*. Up until thirty-four days ago, he had worked for a local mob boss named Ned Wilson, mostly handling Wilson's money laundering activities. But then the cops nailed him in a sting operation for extortion, having him dead to rights with video recordings, and Lutcher, looking at a minimum of ten years in federal prison, agreed to give up his boss.

Lutcher made a face as he spotted the bag from a fast-food joint, but he waited until he was seated at a small table with the two detectives before sharing his thoughts about having greasy burgers and fries for dinner.

"Chrissakes, nothing but franks and beans while we were holed up in that cabin. Four weeks of that. And now that we're in a hotel with room service, we got to eat this crap?"

Souza arched an eyebrow. Weller shook his head. "We're not using room service," he stated adamantly, leaving no room for discussion.

Lutcher unwrapped his burger and his lips folded downward into an almost comical look of disgust. For a moment, he appeared like he wanted to cry.

"For four weeks I've had two grand burning a hole in my wallet," he said. "Let me spend some of it now. Sirloin steak and baked potatoes. Shrimp cocktail. Apple pie with vanilla ice cream. What do you say, gents? All on me."

Souza watched Weller carefully as his partner took a bite of his burger and slowly chewed his food. The detective waited until he swallowed a mouthful of masticated burger before telling Lutcher that that wasn't going to be happening.

"This could be my last meal," Lutcher complained. "Death row inmates get better last meals."

Weller's eyes glazed as he ignored him and kept eating. "How do you figure?" Souza asked.

"I'll be vulnerable tomorrow," Lutcher said. "When I enter the courthouse and when I'm leaving it. Even inside the courtroom I'll be an open target for whoever Ned hired. If his hitman is going to take me out, it will be then. So yeah, this could be my last meal."

"We'll be getting you breakfast tomorrow morning," Weller deadpanned.

"Funny guy, your partner," Lutcher said to Souza. He edged his chair closer to the table and leaned forward, his face twisting into a beseeching look. "If you're going to be all paranoid about room service poisoning my meal, then how about one of you go out and pick up some real takeout? You do that, a hundred buck tip to each of you. How about it?"

Souza again arched an eyebrow toward his partner. Weller, for his part put down his burger and glared at Ned Wilson's onetime underling.

"Are you trying to bribe a police officer?" he said.

Lutcher shrugged his rounded shoulders. "I'm trying to get decent meal," he said.

"Yeah, well, even if we wanted to accommodate you, we can't. Protocol doesn't allow it. So quit your yapping already. All I've been hearing for four weeks has been your yapping, and I'm getting sick of it."

More to himself than to either of the detectives, Lutcher said, "If I have to eat this crap, I think I'll cry."

"I wouldn't recommend that," Souza said, a wiseass smile hardening his lips. "Food won't taste any better soggy."

"Both of you, a pair of comedians," Lutcher said, defeated. "It's like being in Vegas." He picked up his burger, took a bite and made a face as he chewed it. "Maybe if I had a good glass of scotch, I'd be able to stomach this crap. But there's not even a minibar here."

"Our captain had it taken out," Souza explained.

"Goddamned sadist." Lutcher leaned forward and licked his lips as he tried again to implore the detectives. "Room service has a ten-year-old Macallan listed. It's way overpriced, but I'll spring for it, and we can have ourselves a pleasant evening sipping a decent scotch and playing some five-card stud. What do you say, boys? Bottle will be sealed, so no chance of it being poisoned."

Souza gave Weller a questioning look. "Drinking scotch will be better than listening to Henry whine all night," he said. "And as long as the bottle's sealed?"

Weller's resolve weakened. "Anything's worth it to shut this guy up," he said.

Weller called room service and put in a special request that they text him a photo of the waiter bringing them the scotch. If the woman taking the call found anything unusual about the request, she didn't mention it. Five minutes later a photo was texted to Weller, and when room service knocked on the door, Weller looked through the peephole to make sure that the guy was the same person from the photo. Still, Souza stood hidden with his service revolver out while Lutcher stayed in the bedroom.

Weller made sure the bottle of scotch was sealed, then handed the waiter the wad of cash he'd gotten from Lutcher and told him he'd bring the cart into the room himself. The waiter, a skinny kid who looked barely twenty, appeared curious about what was going on, but didn't say anything about the precautions taken. He simply thanked the police detective for the tip and left the room.

Weller left the cart by the door and brought the bottle to the table where they had eaten their fast food. Lutcher had a bounce in his step and a big grin stretched across his face as he exited the bedroom and joined the detectives. Drinks were poured and a poker game was started. They were on their second round of drinks when Weller noticed that Lutcher was slumping forward, his eyes drooping and his round head lolling to one side. The cards fell out of Lutcher's hand, showing that the onetime underling had held a full house, jacks and nines.

"I don't feel so good," Souza said, his speech slurred, his eyes nearly closed. He tried to get out of his chair, but collapsed back onto it. Then he fell to the floor.

Weller wasn't feeling too good either. It was as if his entire face had been injected with Novocain and his limbs disconnected from his body. He tried to blink away a thick shadow darkening his vision, but wasn't sure whether he had succeeded in briefly closing his eyes.

Poisoned, he thought. The whiskey...poisoned. The seal didn't mean shit.

A hissing sound caught his attention. Through the haze he noticed a small hose coming out of the opposite wall. It wasn't the scotch. Someone in the neighboring room had drilled a hole through the wall and was now pumping gas into the room.

Weller felt too weak to stand but was able to fall to the floor. He started crawling toward the door. He needed to get out of the suite and into the hallway so he could breathe in clean air. He made it a couple of feet and then fell into unconsciousness.

It was a minute later that the hose was pulled out of the wall. After that there were several minutes of a pounding sound, and then a sledgehammer broke through the wall. The sledgehammer was pulled back into the adjoining room and then more pieces of the wall were busted off until a hole was made that was large enough for someone to crawl through. The hitman using the sledgehammer wore a gasmask. He tore off more of the wall with his hands to make the hole even bigger and then went through it.

The hotel had been built in the 1920s and still had its original windows, which were the type that could be opened. The hitman opened them wide to bring in fresh air. He had a bag slung over his shoulder, and he took masking tape from it and used it to bind the detectives' wrists and ankles. The gas would leave them with a hellacious headache when they woke up, but nothing worse than that. The hitman, who went by the name Lance, didn't bother gagging them since it would be hours before they'd wake up.

Lance dragged Lutcher by his feet into the bedroom. He then arranged the unconscious man onto a chair and after binding his wrists and ankles together, took a hypodermic needle from his bag and injected a serum into a vein that he found on Lutcher's arm. It only took seconds after that for Lutcher's eyes to flutter open. Lance slapped him until the man woke up completely. At first Lutcher stared dumbly at Lance and then he winced in pain as he understood what was happening.

"You're here to kill me," he groaned, his voice deeper, more guttural than earlier.

"I am," Lance admitted in a soft voice. "To be honest, you were dead the moment Wilson hired me, you just didn't know it yet. I'm not saying that to brag, I'm just telling you the reality of the situation. You will be dying soon. There's nothing you can do to change that. The only thing you can do is control how much pain you suffer before you die."

"What do you mean?"

"Wilson has a list of questions he wants me to ask you. If you answer honestly, you won't needlessly suffer before I shut off your lights. If you lie or are evasive, I will do unspeakable things to you. I won't enjoy doing them, just like I've never enjoyed doing them when I've had to, but I'll be able to live with it as I've always been able to. I should warn you that I'm better than any lie detector and I won't be giving you any second chances. Do you understand what I'm saying?"

Lutcher nodded glumly, tears leaking from his eyes.

Lance took a recorder from his bag and turned it on. He then asked Lutcher the questions that Wilson had given him. He was satisfied with the answers he was given, or more precisely, with Lutcher's truthfulness. At the end, while he was attaching a suppressor to a Smith & Wesson 9mm, Lutcher tried bargaining with him, offering him more money than whatever Wilson was paying him. Lance answered him by firing a bullet into the back of his head. He checked to make sure his target was dead, then left to go back to the adjoining hotel room so he could pack up his gear.

Later, after Wilson paid him what he was owed, Lance was on Interstate 90 East driving back to Chicago when his cell phone rang. Caller ID showed it was Raskins. All he wanted to do right then was get back home, eat a good meal, and hit the hay, and if it had been anyone else he would've ignored the call. But if Raskins was calling, it meant it was really Big Charlie Conaway calling. He answered the call and asked Raskins what he wanted.

"Where are you?" Raskins asked.

"None of your damn business. I don't like repeating myself. What do you want?"

"For you to be in my office tomorrow morning at ten."

"What if I'm busy?"

"Tough."

Lance was somewhat amused and mostly annoyed by Raskins's presumptuousness. He was an independent contractor. He took the meetings he wanted to take and accepted the jobs he wanted to accept. Raskins had never tried strong-arming his before.

"You do realize I'm not in Conaway's employ," he said. "Just because I've done jobs for your boss before doesn't mean

I'll jump every time he snaps his fingers."

"This time you'll jump. The job's urgent. A five-alarm fire. And the big guy is snapping his fingers. Tomorrow morning. Ten a.m. Understood?"

"I don't appreciate your tone."

"I know you don't and I'm sorry. I truly am. But the big guy's not leaving me any choice and he's not leaving you any either. The job's one only you can do, at least that's what he thinks. I can guarantee you'll be happy with the pay."

Lance considered disconnecting the call and sleeping late the next morning, but Conaway had a nasty temper and there was no telling what the guy might do. It would be stupid as hell for Conaway to go to war with him over a perceived slight, but it could happen, and the bloodshed that followed wouldn't be good for anyone.

"What's the job?" he asked.

Raskins chuckled out a raspy sound. "Collecting butterflies," he said.

Marty "The Toad" Raskins was usually as inscrutable and phlegmatic as a two-hundred-and-fifty-pound block of cheese, but at that moment perspiration dotted his forehead and his right eye blinked rapidly with a muscle twitch. For all his bravado on the phone the previous night, he couldn't help the fact that Lance made him nervous. Raskins would have preferred to put anyone else on the job, but even if the boss hadn't demanded it be given to this stone-cold killer, Lance was the guy to call whenever there was an ugly, festering problem that badly needed lancing. The thought occurred to Raskins for the first time that that was how the guy got his moniker since he doubted it was Lance's actual birth name.

Lance, sitting comfortably with his right leg crossed over his left knee, asked, "How about you explain your cryptic message from last night?"

Raskins cleared his throat and said, "We got a girl who needs to be found and then disappeared."

"Is that what you call girls in the wind now? Butterflies?"

"That's not it. This one's got a pink butterfly tattoo on her ass."

In a voice slicker than ice, Lance asked for the girl's name.

"We don't got a name."

"What else?"

"What do you mean what else?"

The way the hitman looked at him made Raskins shiver.

"Give me a description."

"The tattoo's all I got." Raskins thick lips pushed into a scowl creasing the round face that earned him his nickname. Defensively, he added, "That should be enough."

Lance smiled in a way that might've been mistaken as amused, so long as his eyes were ignored. "How about you quit wasting my time and bring Danny Meadows here."

Somehow Raskins managed to keep himself from flinching. He tried to bluff, saying, "Why would I do that?" He knew right away it was a lousy bluff, and from the way Lance smiled at him as if he were dealing with a simpleton, Lance knew it also.

"You're going to make me spell out why one and one equals two, huh? Okay, fine. This has to be wrapped up with the Trevor Haywood hit. Several of your employees have been spreading the word that Haywood was sliced up from head to toe before taking a clip under his chin to make it bloody and brutal, which means it was meant as a message by your boss. It had to be Meadows who did the job for three reasons. First, if it was anyone other than your boss's only nephew, he would've iced the guy instead of engaging in this needle in a haystack hunt for a girl with a butterfly tattoo. Second, Meadows likes using a knife a little too much. And third, Meadows is just dumb enough not to bother checking whether someone's hiding under a bed before going to work and he'd be too caught up in his sadism to notice her escaping, at least until it was too late."

Lance checked his watch, then told Raskins he had fifteen minutes to produce Danny Meadows or find his boss another problem solver for this mess. Raskins began sputtering as if he were planning to argue with Lance over his assumptions, but then his face sagged and he got on the phone.

Thirteen minutes later an angry-looking Meadows entered the room. He took a seat to Lance's right and then complained to Raskins that Lance wasn't supposed to be told about him. "Uncle Charlie promised that," he noted churlishly.

"I didn't tell him nothin'," Raskins explained, red-faced. "He sized up the situation on his own."

Meadows turned to give Lance a slow look up and down, his eyelids dropping as he forced a menacing look. "I know you fancy yourself some badass *mutha*, but if you think I'm afraid of the likes of you, think again, pal."

"Simmer down, boychick. All I want is for you to tell me what you can about this girl."

Meadows's expression shifted from surly to petulant. "How about you go to hell," he said. He started to push himself out of his chair, but Lance clasped onto Meadows's shoulder and forced him back down.

Meadows's face screwed up in pain. Even though he outweighed Lance by sixty pounds, he appeared helpless to break free of Lance's grip.

"You're not thinking about this right," Lance told him in a soft, calm voice. "You need me to find this girl. If I don't, the next job your uncle puts me on will be to make you disappear. He won't have any choice. He can't leave loose ends hanging. Besides, it's not like you're blood, just his wife's sister's kid."

Meadows's eyes widened as he darted a look toward Raskins, showing that this thought hadn't previously occurred to him. Raskins shrugged, his inscrutableness fully back in place. "Anything's possible," he said.

Meadows quit struggling. "You can let go," he said, defeated. "I'll tell you what I can, which isn't much other than that tattoo.

I only caught a glimpse of her from behind as she ran out of there."

"How'd that happen?"

"I don't know." Meadows clamped his lips so tightly together that the muscles along his jaw bulged. "She must've crawled out of bed and crouched down low enough so I couldn't see her, and then hid herself. I guess she waited for her chance to bolt and took it when I was otherwise preoccupied."

"She ran out of there naked?"

"As a jaybird. She had her clothes and pocketbook bundled up, but she hadn't put anything on. Which is why I saw the butterfly tattoo."

"Wings open or closed?"

"What?"

"The butterfly. Tell me about the design."

"Wings were open."

"What side was it on?"

Meadows's eyes dulled as he thought about it. "With her facing away from me, it was on her right ass cheek."

"Any special detail?"

"Nothing. Just that it was pink."

Lance let it drop. No matter how hard he tried, he wasn't about to get a better description of the tattoo from Meadows. "She leave anything behind?" he asked.

"Her shoes." Meadows gave Lance a knowing glance. "I got rid of them. I didn't want the cops looking for a possible witness."

Of course the putz did. Lance knew what Meadows's answer would be, but he asked anyway about the brand and shoe size.

"Who cares about that? They were just shoes. Nothing special about them."

"Where'd you toss them?"

"In a furnace. I watched them burn. The cops aren't finding them, if that's what's worrying you."

Too dumb to live. That was all Lance could think. He didn't belabor the point that the shoes might've given him a better chance to find the girl than the tattoo.

"What about Haywood's phone?"

"What about it?"

"It might've had the woman's name and address in it. So I'm assuming you took Haywood's phone before you left."

"I looked for it, but couldn't find it."

That was a lie. Lance could tell that from the way's Meadows's eyes had glazed. The dumb ox never thought of taking Haywood's phone. Homicide would have it now and not even Conaway would have enough juice to get the phone back.

He asked, "Other than the tattoo, what can you tell me about her?"

"Nothing. As I said, she was out of there in a flash." Meadows scrunched his eyes as he gave it more thought. "I have an impression of her being white, in her twenties, blond, and thin. On the short side. Around five feet two. But I could be wrong about all of that."

"You were just fixated on the tattoo?"

"For the split second I saw her, yeah."

"Why didn't you chase after her?"

"My gloves were too slick with blood. I had to burn time getting them off before I could open the door. She was gone by the time I got out of the bedroom. I found an open window leading to an alley. She must've climbed out of it. I had to finish up with Haywood since she could've been sending the cops there any minute, and afterward I searched the alley and the neighborhood, but no luck. Like I said before, I got nothing useful to tell."

Lance had to admit when the *schmuck* was right, he was right. Meadows had nothing to give him. He got to his feet. On his way out the door, he told Raskins he'd be in touch about this impossible assignment.

* * *

25

There were seventeen tattoo parlors in the city and neighboring suburbs, and Lance hired a freelancer he occasionally used, Nellie Hannigan, to get what she could out of them. It took her three days to report back to him that what she got was bupkes.

"All the parlors have butterfly tattoo designs, and I gave the artists working at these parlors an innocent story—that I had a recent drunken hookup, but all I knew about her was the tattoo, and I was desperate to find her since it was the hottest sex I've ever had. I made it worth their while to help me, and unless I read them wrong, they all wanted to, but none of them remembered inking a pink butterfly on a girl's bottom."

"Girl's *bottom*," Lance repeated, smiling. "Refined language for a hit woman."

"No reason to be indelicate. And I like to think of myself as a consultant dealing with intractable problems. Back to the matter at hand—if you'd like I could extend the search to the rest of the state and beyond. But it's possible the general description you have of the subject is wrong, in which case I doubt I'll trigger any memories with these artists. None of the parlors I visited kept records of the tattoos they give their clients, so even if I find an artist who remembers inking your butterfly, there's a snowball's chance the person will be able to provide a name."

Lance agreed that it didn't seem worth the effort or Nellie's talents, and paid her what he owed her.

He knew from the start the tattoo parlor angle had only a small chance of paying off, at best, and so he'd been busy the past three days, first seeing whether anyone spotted a naked woman in the alley Meadows had pointed out, and then digging into Trevor Haywood's background. While he couldn't find where Haywood had spent the last evening of his life, he discovered that Haywood favored a particular type; namely slender blondes, and that he was old-fashioned in that he didn't use technology for his hookups, but preferred the challenge of picking up a woman at a bar. Lance also had the names of a half dozen establishments Haywood liked to frequent, most of which were in or near the Bronzeville neighborhood. While it was disconcerting that none of the bartenders at these places remembered seeing Haywood his last evening alive, it wasn't necessarily a dead-end. Haywood could've met the girl with the pink butterfly tattoo another night and arranged to meet up with her at his apartment. He'd been a good-looking guy, but in a way which would allow him to blend into a crowd of other good-looking guys on the make, so it was easy to imagine a bartender not noticing him on a busy night.

After Lance's meeting with Nellie, he went back to his apartment and stripped down to his boxers. He had bought a kit for a temporary pink butterfly tattoo, and when he was done applying it to his right bicep, he had to admit the resulting tattoo looked like the real thing. Earlier he had worn a conservative suit, and now he put on more stylish clothes, which included a tight short sleeve knit shirt which would show off his new tattoo. He slipped on a leather jacket and headed to one of the bars on his list. What he was thinking was a longshot at best, but it was all he had.

It was early enough for him to get a seat at the bar. He took off his jacket and was still nursing his first beer when he felt someone touching his arm. He turned to see a very pretty woman lightly tracing the butterfly on his bicep with her well-manicured index finger. She gave him a cat-who-swallowed-a-canary smile and told him that she was admiring his tattoo. Her smile grew more impish as she noted, "It seems like an odd choice for someone like you."

The woman, as well as being very attractive, was young and slender, but she wasn't a blonde. Instead she had dark brown hair which matched the color of her eyebrows. But that didn't necessarily mean anything. Even if Meadows was right, what he saw could've been a dye job. Haywood was killed over a week ago, which would've given the girl with the butterfly tattoo more than enough time to dye her hair back to its natural color, and she would've wanted to do that, especially if she was worried a hit man might be looking for a blond witness.

He smiled at her. "I lost a bet. How about you? Do you have hidden ink that might surprise me?"

She leaned in close to him so she could whisper in his ear. "I might. And if you're really lucky tonight, you might even get to see it."

Lance bought her several drinks and later that night was taken back to her apartment. He was lucky to a point. He got to see all her tattoos, but there were no butterflies.

Over the next four days Lance visited different bars from Haywood's list of favorites, and each night he had a woman who could be the blonde he was looking for express amusement over his butterfly tattoo. As with his first night, the woman would hint that she had private ink she might show him if the night went well, but in none of these cases did the tattoo turn out to be a butterfly. On the fifth day, he got a call from Raskins who told him that the big boss wasn't happy that Lance hadn't gotten the job done yet.

"He has unrealistic expectations," Lance growled back. "Your boss should change the job and let me get rid of his idiot nephew instead. That would make a hell of a lot more sense."

"I talked with him about that and it's not an option. You got one week to get this done."

"Or else, huh?"

Raskins let out a soft, raspy noise that could've been him chuckling. "No one ever said you weren't bright," he said.

"It's an impossible job," Lance complained.

"You're supposed to be able to handle these impossible jobs. Figure it out."

Raskins hung up leaving Lance fuming and staring at his phone. That fat toad wouldn't have had the guts to speak to him directly like that if they'd been face to face, but distance had given him courage. Lance took several deep breaths in an attempt to calm himself down. He needed to be relaxed and easygoing if he was going to use his pink butterfly tattoo later that evening to lure its counterpart. He took one last deep breath and held it for a ten-count before letting the air out slowly through his nose, all the while thinking about the girl with the pink butterfly tattoo who had so far eluded him.

Of course, he always had the option of *disappearing* any young blonde who fit the bill. The job required him to provide, among other things, photographic evidence of the girl's tattoo, but he could use the same kit he had bought for himself and apply it to whatever girl he chose. The idea of doing that, though, sickened him and went against his fundamental core principle of never causing any collateral damage. That was the code he lived by and he'd be damned if he'd change it now for any reason, even self-preservation.

As hard as he tried to forget it, Raskins call left him in a rotten mood, and even though it was hours later, he needed several drinks that night before he loosened up enough to become approachable. At least that's how many it took before the first woman came over to comment about his butterfly tattoo. He gave her a quick glance. She was cute and the right age, but too plump to be the girl he was looking for.

"You like it, huh?" he said, trying not to sound encouraging.

"I do," the woman said. "I think a friend of mine will like it even more. Would you mind if I text her and see if she's available?"

"Not at all."

The woman's thumbs were a blur as she texted out a message on her cellphone at a speed that surpassed anything a person Lance's age could ever muster. The response to her text made the woman's brow furrow, but after a flurry of more texts her face brightened.

"My friend can be here in a half hour if you'll wait?" the woman asked.

"Happily."

That made the woman's face brighten even more. "She's been so down in the dumps lately," she said. "This will cheer her up."

The woman introduced herself as Susan, and while they waited, Lance bought her a drink and chatted her up. Susan didn't know why her friend was so down, but over the last few days, maybe even longer, she'd seemed overly preoccupied as if something were troubling her. "Toni's such a sweet person. I hate seeing her like this." Susan took another look at Lance's butterfly tattoo and smiled secretively as she added, "Maybe the two of you were meant for each other."

Lance didn't bother asking why that would be. He didn't need her to tell him the obvious as he knew his longshot would soon be paying off. Susan was in the middle of telling him a story about Toni when she looked past him and waved enthusiastically. She then bolted off her barstool and rushed to meet her friend. Once the two women finished hugging, Lance got a clear look at Toni. She had chestnut brown hair, but otherwise fit the bill. About twenty-five, slender, on the short side, and cute. Actually more beautiful than cute with her slightly upturned nose dotted with freckles, large hazel-colored eyes, and delicate chin. As the two women approached him, Lance could see Toni's blond roots. The chestnut brown was a dye job, probably done within a week. So Danny Meadows had been right about the target being blond.

He smiled and held out his hand. She reciprocated, and her hand felt small inside of his own, almost like a child's.

"Frank," he said, using the name he'd had a different lifetime ago. "And you must be Toni? Damn, you don't look like any Tony I've ever known."

That got her blushing. "Toni is short for Antoinette," she said.

"Of course. A beautiful name."

She scrunched up her cute, slightly upturned nose at that. "I never really cared for it, hence Toni." Her lips twisted into a thin smile. "I'll bet you a drink you're ex-military."

Lance laughed at that. A genuine one. "Special forces for eight years," he told her, which was true. "How'd you know that?"

"My dad was in the army." Her smile dimmed in a way that told Lance her dad hadn't retired, but instead left the service in a box. "As a former military brat, I've gotten very good at spotting other military. And you have to be ex since you're dressed way too nicely to be active duty."

"*Nicely* being a euphemism for expensively."

"Exactly."

Susan piped in, saying, "Smart as a whip, isn't she."

Lance's attention had been so laser-focused on Toni that he had forgotten the other woman was there. "No doubt about that." Lance waved the bartender over so he could order another round of drinks for himself and Susan, and whatever Toni wanted. She asked for a bourbon neat, which Lance respected.

"Your friend seems like a nice guy," Toni told Susan. She didn't say the word *but*; she didn't need to since it was implied by the questioning tone in her voice, as if she was wondering why her friend had insisted she come to the bar.

"You haven't noticed yet what's on Frank's right arm?" Susan said, barely able to contain her glee.

Toni did then, and she burst out laughing. Susan joined in.

"I'm glad I can be so amusing," Lance said as if his feelings were hurt. His pink butterfly lure had worked, and he knew what he'd see if he removed Toni's tight jeans and panties, but he had to play a certain part, and so he did.

"I'm sorry," Toni said when she could. "It's a private joke."

Lance exaggerated a harrumphing noise. "Maybe you can let me in on it since I seem to be the *butt* of it."

That got Toni laughing so uproariously she had to wipe tears from her eyes. Nearly out of breath, she said, "I'm not laughing at you. I swear. I'd tell you the joke, but it would be embarrassing." Her eyes glistened as she grinned wickedly at Lance. "Maybe once I get to know you better."

"I would not be opposed to that."

"My cue to leave," Susan said. She hugged Toni, winked at Lance, and walked away looking only a little tipsy from the three gimlets Lance had bought her.

It was still early enough for them to move to an open table, and they spent the next three hours eating, drinking, and talking about their lives, although Lance brushed past what he'd been doing since leaving the military, describing it only as consulting on unusual problems. He learned that Toni's last name was Bonnard, she was in fact twenty-five, she'd moved to the city for college, and that she was a second-grade teacher at a nearby elementary school. When she pressed him about why he got the butterfly tattoo, he told her that he liked to tell people it was because of a bet he lost, but it was really because of a crazy dream.

"I like crazy dreams," she said.

"Then you'll like this one. I dreamt that I would only find my true love if I got this tattoo. Crazy, huh? The thing was, I couldn't shake the thought that there was something behind it. And so, the butterfly on my arm."

He could see in her eyes that that almost loosened her up enough to tell him about her own butterfly tattoo, but she held back and he understood why. She was afraid someone like him could be looking for her. He was impressed at how perceptive she was even if she dismissed the idea of him being that guy as too outlandish. At the end of the evening, she told him that she needed this evening out more than he would ever know. She smiled mischievously and added, "I'm really glad I met you, Frank, and not just because of the pink butterfly on your arm."

"You're still not going to let me in on the joke, huh?"

Her smile turned coy. "Another day, perhaps."

"How about tomorrow? At least let me buy you dinner and we can see if that leads to me coaxing your secret out of you."

"Deal!"

They exchanged phone numbers—Lance had brought a burner phone with him for exactly this contingency—and they made plans on when and where to meet the following night. He asked whether she'd like him to escort her home and she hesitated before telling him that she lived nearby and she'd be fine by herself. So she still wasn't a hundred percent sure he wasn't a guy hired to hunt her down. Again, he admired her perceptiveness.

He waited several minutes after she left the bar before going after her. It was easy enough for him to pick up her trail and follow her to a four-story tenement building; the type of place he'd expect someone with a schoolteacher's salary to be able to afford. Once she was out of sight he entered the building's lobby and found her mailbox. It just had her name on it which meant she didn't have a roommate. He could break into her apartment now, verify that she had the tattoo he knew she had to have, and finish the business tonight. But there was a one in a million chance she wasn't his target, and he wasn't about to make Toni collateral damage, especially since he'd had a hard time reconciling her as being one of Trevor Haywood's hookups even though he knew that had to be the case. He reminded himself there was no reason to be in a rush. He'd been given a week to finish the job, so he could wait another day for Toni to tell him her secret. He took a cab back to his Lakeview apartment.

He had trouble sleeping later that night. All of his previous targets deserved what happened to them. Toni was something very different; an innocent who had the bad luck of being in the wrong place at the wrong time. But, as Lance kept telling himself, plenty of people die for no other reason than bad luck, even ones as cute and innocent as Toni Bonnard. Besides, how innocent could she really be if she hooked up with a scumbag like Trevor Haywood?

None of this rationalizing helped ease his mind. At times he'd flash back to earlier that evening and he'd picture Toni with her slightly upturned nose and the way she looked at him with such earnestness. Yeah, he was attracted to her. How messed up was that? He also knew that the attraction wasn't a one-way street; although with her it was more than that. He had seen the relief wash over her the moment she realized he was ex-military. It made her feel safe, like he'd protect her the same as her dad had once done, and that thought in particular brought up something sour in Lance's stomach.

He swung himself out of bed, accepting that he wasn't going to sleep given his current state of mind. Whatever Toni was, she was a target, and Big Charlie Conaway had a legit reason for needing her to disappear. None of it might've been fair, but it didn't matter. Lance would verify that she had the butterfly tattoo on her butt and he would do his job, although he'd be more gentle with her than his other targets and would drug her so she would never know what happened.

Accepting that all this was inevitable helped calm down his thoughts. He lay back in bed, and this time he dozed off.

The next evening he met Toni at their agreed upon place, and while the job required him to put on an act, he didn't have to try all that hard. She looked so vulnerable, so heart-achingly beautiful. She seemed to sense the effect she was having on him and teased him about it.

"You're just trying to worm my secret out of me."

"Is it working?"

"It just might be."

Toni seemed mostly buoyant that evening, as if she believed she had survived a great ordeal and better times were on the horizon, but at times she'd become distracted. Those moments didn't last long as she'd shake herself out of the dark thoughts plaguing her. After one of these moments, she confided to Lance that she was thinking about leaving the city.

"I grew up on Army bases, and so when it was time to go to college I thought it would be exciting to move here, but now all I can think about is going someplace out West. Someplace like Wyoming or Montana with wide open spaces where I could just disappear under a big sky."

"Yeah, sometimes I think about getting in a car and driving far away and never coming back," Lance said, playing along.

Toni showed a sad smile. "Except I don't have a car."

She shook herself out of her temporary funk and was soon

buoyant again. After they finished dinner and she arranged for a ride back to her apartment, she told Lance he could kiss her. He took her up on her offer.

"You still owe me a secret," he said, his voice surprisingly froggy.

She smiled at the obvious effect she had on him. "Another day."

"The suspense is killing me."

"Poor baby. Be patient."

He arched an eyebrow. "So just the one kiss, huh?"

She put a small, delicate hand on his cheek. "For now," she said.

He had a vial of Rohypnol in his pocket, but that would just have to wait. He stayed with Toni until her ride came and waved to her as her car drove off.

Lance saw Toni each of the next four nights, and the first three of them went pretty much the same as their first one. After dinner they'd share a kiss, the duration of which grew with each successive night, and with half-lidded eyes and a throaty voice Toni would ask him to be patient and he'd watch as an Uber ride would drive her away. He considered on the fourth night slipping Rohypnol into her wine so that he'd have to escort her home, but he still had two days so he decided to hold off. He was rewarded later when following their after-dinner kiss she invited him back to her apartment. "I'm finally ready to show you my secret," she said, her voice throatier than any time earlier.

"We should celebrate this evening with champagne," he said. Toni agreed, and so he had their driver stop off at a liquor store. Lance paid cash for the champagne, just as he had done with dinner and with the cabdriver. He wasn't about to leave a paper trail.

During the ride back to her apartment, he decided he needed to be a hundred percent sure that she was the target he needed to disappear. Simply seeing the butterfly tattoo wouldn't be enough. Once they were alone in her small one-bedroom apartment, she asked if he'd like to open the champagne.

"Maybe we can sit first?"

"Excellent suggestion."

They sat together on a sofa and kissed for several minutes. When they separated for air, Lance held her gently by the shoulders and looked deeply into her eyes.

"Something's troubling you," he said. "I've seen glimpses of it since I first met you. Please, tell me what it is and maybe I can help."

She crumbled then, her face all of a sudden a mask of pain. "Something terrible happened." Her voice was choked with emotion. "I never had a one-night hookup before, but after the school year ended two weeks ago I was celebrating and I made an awful mistake...I went back with a stranger to his apartment and something terrible happened...Something unimaginable...I don't know what to do."

She was shaking. He held her tight and shushed her and told her she didn't need to tell him anything more. He couldn't quite remember how he had ended up on the path he did. When he left the military, he mostly stumbled into this work. He was good at it and never disappointed a client. Big Charlie Conaway had a good reason for wanting Toni to disappear and Lance couldn't blame him for hiring him to do the job, but he decided to take on a new client, namely himself. As he hugged Toni and tried to sooth her, he made a mental list of the people he'd have to take out so he'd be able to continue seeing Toni and the two of them would be safe. Aside from Conaway, Meadows, and Raskins, there were four other people he needed to terminate. He would have only two days and the timing of the hits would be tight, but he would figure out a way to get the job done. One thing he knew for sure, he wasn't about to cry over any of them. They all deserved what would be happening to them.

"Everything's going to be okay. I promise." He kissed her hard and tasted the saltiness of her tears. He felt a catch in his throat as he whispered to her that he shouldn't be there. "I've got a project with a near-impossible deadline that I should be spending all my time on, but it's been so damn hard to resist you. Here's a crazy idea. Give me two days to finish the job, and then I'll get a car and drive us out West. Anywhere you want to go. And we never have to come back."

She pulled away from him so she could search his eyes. "Are you serious?" she asked.

"As serious as I've ever been."

A sad smile twisted her lips. "I think I like crazy ideas even more than crazy dreams."

He kissed her one last time and forced himself off the sofa. Plans were already formulating in his mind. He'd worked out an order so he'd be able to take out all of the targets he needed to remove before any of them realized what was happening. He'd also make their bodies disappear so that when he disappeared it would be assumed that he had gotten taken out along with the rest of them. If somehow a new organization rose from the ashes, there'd be no reason for anyone to look for him. First things first, he'd find an open tattoo parlor and make his butterfly permanent so Toni wouldn't be wondering in a week why his ink was fading away. After that, he'd visit Danny Meadows and start the ball rolling.

When he got to the door, he promised her he'd be back in two days. "Be packed and ready to go, okay?"

"I'll be ready." She showed him more of her sad smile. "I didn't get a chance to reveal my secret."

He nodded. As much as he wanted to see her tattoo, he would have to be patient. He would also have to find new work soon, but that was more than okay with him. He had a duffel bag stuffed with money hidden in his apartment that he'd use to buy a legit business—maybe a restaurant, maybe something else. In two days, he'd be picking Toni up and then he'd have a whole lifetime to spend with her and her pink butterfly.

He walked out the door knowing that nothing was going to keep him from that.

* * *

The next day Lance arranged to meet with Nellie Hannigan at a shopping center parking lot outside the city limits. When she got into his car, she commented on his butterfly tattoo.

"That looks like the real thing," she said as she ran a finger over his tattoo.

"It is."

"What happened? You spent so much time searching for that pink butterfly, you decided you needed one for yourself?"

"Something like that."

Her smile faded as her expression became more somber. "This must be serious if you want to meet out here in the boondocks."

"It is. I'm taking out Conaway and six others. I need your help."

"Wow. This isn't a joke, is it?"

"If it is, it's not a funny one. At least I don't have a punchline for it."

"Again, wow," she said. "I'm flattered, I guess, that you trust me enough to tell me this. Of course, if I were to double-cross you, the odds are I'd end up dead or worse. Still, I'm flattered. Who's the client?"

"I am."

Nellie's eyes narrowed to slits as she studied Lance. "You found her," she said at last. "That's why you got that ridiculous tattoo. To use as bait. But you didn't carry out the contract." She laughed mirthlessly and her smile didn't come close to reaching her eyes. "Are you always willing to go on a suicide mission whenever you fall hard for a dame?"

"I can't say. This is the first it's happened. But it's not a suicide mission. By this time tomorrow I'll be done and gone. As I said, I need your help. So name your price."

"What about the blowback?"

"There won't be any. I guarantee it."

"What if you make a mistake and get yourself caught?

There's a first time for everything, right?"

"It won't happen," Lance said. "But if it did, you really think there's anything they could do to me for me to give up your name?"

Nellie didn't need long to think that over. "No, I suppose not," she said. "But I want to know why there won't be blowback."

Lance explained his reason and more specifically what he needed her to do, and when he was done she gave him a price of fifty grand.

"I know that's a lot, but this is pretty high-priced shit you're asking for," she said.

"Not all that high under the circumstances. I'll be right back."

Lance left the car so he could take fifty grand from the duffel bag in his trunk. The money he took out barely made a dent. When he returned, he handed Nellie the money.

"You realize that in the long run I'm going to lose business from this," she said. "Conaway was always good for at least three contracts a year."

"You won't lose anything," Lance said. "The players might change, but the game won't. Whoever takes over Conaway's businesses will be throwing jobs your way. And you'll have less competition since I'll be retiring to parts unknown."

Lance took out a notepad and went into more details about his plan. When he was done, Nellie told him the schedule he drew up would be tight but doable. She checked the time and told him it could be a few hours before he'd be hearing from her, which was what Lance expected. She gave him a funny, almost wistful smile as she left the car. "I guess after tomorrow I won't be seeing you again," she said.

"You'll have that fifty grand to remember me by," he said.

Lance had already done most of the prep work, but there were still a few things to do before Nellie made contact with their first victim, and so he drove back to Chicago. The hour ride went by quickly, his mind drifting and long stretches of time disappearing on him. When he got back to his apartment, he used a knife blade to slit open his palm, and then smeared blood through his apartment as if there'd been a struggle. Once that was done, he got out his special first aid kit, stitched up his hand, then wrapped a bandage over it. After that, he cooked up a plate of spaghetti and sausages, ate half of it, then knocked over his chair and the table he'd been using, sending what was left of his meal crashing to the floor. Maybe his downstairs neighbors heard the ruckus, maybe they didn't, but it wouldn't matter. He was leaving behind all his possessions other than the duffel bag stuffed with money and a change of clothing, and when the cops investigated the only reasonable conclusion they'd be able to make is that he was violently abducted.

Lance left his apartment for what would be the last time and took the fire stairs down to the ground level. He then walked three blocks to where he had left the used car he'd bought earlier that morning under his birth name, which was a name he hadn't used since he got out of the army and that nobody in Chicago knew. He had no bank account, no credit cards, and had worked out a deal where he paid his lease in cash one year in advance. The cops were going to have their work cut out for them to figure out which of his aliases to use when they later reported his disappearance and presumptive murder. While there were no photos of him left in the apartment, his description would be enough to convince the surviving members of the Conaway organization that he had also met a violent end that day.

He drove within two blocks of where Nellie would be bringing his first victim that night and found an empty storefront to park behind. He closed his eyes and concentrated on the details of his plan and played out in his mind what would be happening later. He then thought about all of the things that could go wrong, and the contingencies he'd need to make if any of that happened. He was still doing this when his cell phone chirped, letting him know that Nellie had made contact with their first victim and was bringing him to their agreed upon location. He opened his eyes and was surprised at how much darker it had gotten. A quick check of his phone showed that it was already nine-thirty. Nellie's text message was simply the number twenty, which meant that she and Meadows were twenty minutes away.

The motel room door opened and Nellie walked in first with Danny Meadows following behind. Meadows, a big, dumb grin stretched across his face, took three steps into the room and then stopped to look down at the floor, confused as to why the carpeting was covered with a plastic tarp. That was when Lance used a leather sap to knock Meadows to one knee. Before he could get up, Lance wrapped a barbed wire garrote around his neck. Not much longer after that Meadows was dead.

Nellie had taken off the wig and granny glasses that she had used as part of her disguise. "Charming fella," she said. "A shame to see him taken out by those ruthless *Kamene Ruke*."

The *Kamene Ruke*, which translated roughly to "Hands of Stone," was a Croatian gang, and their signature for executions was the barbed wire garrote. Over the last few months they'd been encroaching on Conaway's businesses, and Conaway had recently responded by having two of their men killed. While the others would disappear that night, Lance would leave Meadows body to be found and the cops would draw the obvious conclusion as to what happened to Big Charlie Conaway and the top brass in his organization.

"Hard bastards, those Croatians," Lance agreed. He searched Meadows's pockets and found his cell phone, then pressed Meadows's index finger against the fingerprint reader to unlock the phone. "Bingo," he said, and he showed Nellie several of the names listed in Meadows's contacts.

"That should make things easier tonight," she said.

"It should," he agreed.

It wouldn't matter if the cops found Meadows in the motel

room as long as it happened tomorrow, but it would screw things up if he were found before then. While it was doubtful that housecleaning would enter the motel room that night, Lance still couldn't take that chance. Nellie waited in the room while he brought back his car. When he returned, he first cut off Meadows's index finger so he'd be able to unlock Meadows's cell phone when needed, then wrapped Meadows up in the plastic tarp and, with a few grunts, deadlifted the two-hundred-and-forty-pound corpse onto his shoulder. Nellie kept a lookout as Lance got the body into his car trunk. It was a tight squeeze, and Lance had moments where he thought he would have to bring Meadows back into the motel room and saw off his legs, but after a few minutes of sweat he was able to get the trunk closed.

"That was a tight fit," Nellie observed, then waved goodbye as she headed off to take care of the next part of her assignment. Lance waited unit he was ten minutes away from the abandoned warehouse before using Meadows's phone to text Conaway's three top lieutenants. Angry texts were sent back and forth with all three of them, but in the end they all showed up together, parking next to the van as they had been instructed. None of them appeared happy as they got out of the car. All three of them, though, seemed surprised when Lance stepped out of the shadows pointing a Browning 9mm at them. The gun had a suppressor attached, and the three shots Lance fired made more of a *puff* sound than a gunshot, but each of the men still dropped dead to the pavement. Lance piled them like firewood into the van that he had stolen the previous night. He used a flashlight to find his spent shell casings and pocketed them. He left his car where he had parked it on the other side of the warehouse, and drove off in the van, which along with the three men he had just killed also held Meadows's body.

Over the last few years Big Charlie Conaway had gotten careless, thinking himself invincible, and had fallen into predictable patterns. Lance had a good idea where Conaway might be at eleven on a Thursday night, and at the fourth place he tried he spotted Conaway's car, along with the mob boss's bodyguard, outside of the East Sixty-first townhouse where Conaway kept his mistress. Lance pulled up alongside the bulletproof Lincoln Continental. Conaway's bodyguard, who was sitting in the driver's seat, turned to give Lance a menacing look, at least until he recognized that Lance was driving.

Lance rolled down a side window so he could have a word with the bodyguard. The bodyguard did likewise.

"I've been looking for your boss," Lance said. "I've got a very special butterfly inside the van that I thought he'd like to see."

"Yeah, you found her?"

"I did. A gorgeous drop-dead knockout. And blond everywhere." Lance lowered his voice and winked at the other man. "I got her tied up on a mattress, and I thought with all the money Big Charlie was paying to find her that he might like to spend some time with her before I make her disappear for good."

The other man made a disappointed grimace. "If you called him an hour ago, maybe. But you know where Mr. Conaway is now, and the man is sixty-two, after all. A shame, though. Especially if she's as nice as you're saying."

Lance grinned. "Nicer," he said.

The man licked his lips. "Mind if I take a look?"

"Not at all."

Lance met the other man at the back of the van, and gestured for the bodyguard to open the door. Lance waited until the other man had done this before knocking him out with the same leather sap he had used on Meadows. Lance then got into the van, pulled the man's unconscious body into it, and shut the door behind him. He put on the bodyguard's Cubs cap and leather jacket, pocketed the Lincoln Continental's car keys, and then with the suppressor still attached to the Browning, fired a bullet into the bodyguard's ear.

A half hour later Conaway left the townhome. He didn't realize that Lance was masquerading as his bodyguard until Lance, who had left the Lincoln presumably to get the door for

Conaway, pointed the Browning at Conaway's chest.

"What the hell is this?" Conaway growled, his face turning beet red.

Lance ignored him. "You see that van?" he asked, referring to the vehicle that he had parked half a block away so as not to draw Conaway's attention earlier. "Start walking to it."

"Screw you."

Lance shot twice him in the chest and Big Charlie Conaway crumpled to the sidewalk. Lance could have left the mob boss where he fell, except it would ruin his Croatian mob story. It was after twelve, the neighborhood was residential, and he hadn't seen anyone walking their dog or otherwise outside. He went back to the van, backed it up, and added Charlie's three-hundred-pound body to the others.

Nellie had called while he was waiting for Conaway, and he drove back to the abandoned warehouse to meet her. She was leaning against the trunk of her car when he pulled the van up next to her. When he got out, she opened the trunk to show Raskins bound and gagged, the fat man's eyes bulging as he struggled fruitlessly to free himself.

"Squirming like a toad," Nellie remarked.

"He's still alive," Lance said.

"Just in case you had anything you wanted to ask him."

Lance had nothing to ask Raskins. He dumped him onto pavement before shooting him, then stored his body with the others.

Nellie joined Lance in the van, and the first stop was back at the motel where Meadows was killed. Nellie got in Meadows's car and drove it while Lance followed in the van. She found a darkened stretch of road thanks to a broken streetlight and parked there. Nellie helped him as Lance got Meadows's corpse behind the wheel. With that taken care of, he drove them back to the warehouse so Nellie could retrieve her car, and then she followed him to South Bend, Indiana.

Lance had made a deal with an employee at a South Bend

crematorium a few years back. Every six months Lance paid the employee twenty grand, and the employee made sure Lance had the security code and keys for the place so he could use it as he wished when the place would normally be closed at night. He and Nellie arrived at the crematorium a little before three in the morning, and since he was able to use all four ovens, by six o'clock they were heading back to Chicago with the Conaway organization reduced to ashes. Lance found a rural stretch of road to torch the van, and then rode with Nellie as she drove him back to the warehouse so he could pick up his car.

"So this is it," Nellie said after dropping him off.

"It would seem so."

"I hope she's worth it."

"She is," Lance said.

Part Three: Antoinette Bonnard, aka Toni, aka The Girl with the Pink Butterfly Tattoo

Lance's clothing was caked with dirt and dried blood when he knocked on Toni's door. It was hard to kill seven people, including one with a garrote, and dispose of their bodies without getting dirty. Toni's eyes widened as she looked at him, but she didn't say anything when he told her that he needed to take a shower and that she should have her bags packed by the time he was done. It wasn't until he was out of the shower and in the change of clothing that he had brought that she mentioned how he had told her the last time they were together that everything would be okay.

"It is."

"It really is safe for me now?"

"There's nobody out there looking to hurt you. Not anymore. But still, we should leave Chicago. Do you still want to go to Montana?"

Tears flooded her eyes. "Yes," she said. She smiled in a way that tugged at Lance's heart. She rushed over to him, embracing him, and then stood on her toes and almost kissed him hard enough to loosen teeth.

"We better get going," Lance said.

She had packed only a single suitcase, and he carried it to his car.

They drove in quiet after that, but it was a comfortable quiet. At times Toni would find his right hand and squeeze it hard. When they stopped at a diner in Rochester, Minnesota, Toni told him she had a confession to make. "I'm not a brunette," she said. "I'm a blonde. I dyed my hair before because I was so worried."

Lance laughed at that. "It doesn't matter what color your hair is." He realized then that it had been almost twenty-four hours since he last ate and that he was damn hungry. He called the waitress over and ordered their steak special. Toni ordered the turkey club.

"This is like a dream," she said after the waitress left. "We're really doing this. Starting a new life together where no-body knows us. What are we going to do in Montana?"

"We could buy a farm," he said. "Or a bar. Or really anything we want to do."

"How about a café?" she asked. "Something cute and inti-mate?"

"We could do that," Lance said.

Toni got excited about buying a café, and she told Lance about her ideas, and he couldn't help smiling over how passionate she had become. Later, when they were back on the Interstate, she asked him what type of family he wanted.

"What do you mean?"

"Do you want children?"

"I've never really thought about that before," he said, which was true. "How about you?"

"I'd like to have them. Ideally four. Two boys and two girls."

"That actually sounds nice."

Toni continued talking about her dreams and hopes for their future life together, which only endeared her more to him. When they found a motel in Sioux Falls, Toni asked him if he could get them a room while she found a liquor store. "We never had that champagne the other night and we really should celebrate our new life together."

Lance didn't hesitate to hand over his car keys or bother taking the duffel bag with him. He told her he'd text her their room number, and handed her two hundred dollars to buy them something good. She rewarded his trust by returning twenty minutes later with a bottle of Dom Perignon.

"I know this is extravagant," she said. "But this is a special night for us."

Lance opened the bottle and poured champagne into two of the motel's plastic cups. Over the next half hour they sat together on a couch and drank half the bottle. Toni suddenly got up and stared at Lance in an odd, calculating kind of way. Lance tried to get off the couch also, but he collapsed back onto it.

"You drugged me," he said, his voice slurred.

"I did. Rohypnol. I should get a standing ovation for the performance I've been giving. I didn't move to Chicago for college and I've certainly never been a schoolteacher," she said as she cautiously watched him. "The reason I went back with Trevor Haywood wasn't because of a drunken hookup. It was because I'd been hearing stories of him ripping off his boss, and I wanted to steal his money. But my rotten luck, that sadistic creep Danny Meadows had to show up. And I knew he saw my butterfly tattoo, which left me screwed. There were too many guys in Chicago who knew about my tattoo, and if I took a powder then, one of those bright boys would've put two and two together and let Big Charlie Conaway know I was the one he was after. So all I could do was dye my hair, stay holed up in my apartment, and pray that Conaway played it close to the vest and didn't let it circulate that he was looking for a blonde with a special insect tattooed on her ass."

Lance's mouth felt so damn cottony. He opened it wide as if he were about to start gagging. "So now you're bragging," he forced out with disgust.

"I'm really not," Antoinette Bonnard said. "I've been terrified of you ever since I saw you. I've heard the stories and I know all about you. Right now I'm having an adrenaline rush like you wouldn't believe, and so I'm rambling. You see, most of my friends live on the same shady side of the street as myself, but I have a few friends, like Susan, who are aboveboard citizens, and I knew when I got her text that it was a trap and she was with one of Conaway's hitmen, and if I didn't show up she'd give me up without knowing any better. My only hope was to play innocent and try to turn the tables on my would-be assassin. When I saw it was you, I knew I was dead, but somehow I made you, stone-cold killer Lance, fall in love with me."

"I've got one and a half million in my car. You can just take it and leave."

"I know about the money," she said. "I found it when I went out for the champagne. I've never killed anyone before, and I really don't want to kill you, but if I took off now you'd hunt me down and kill me. Which is what you do better than anyone else. Which is the only reason you trusted me earlier with your car and that money."

Lance sprang at her. Even though she had been cautiously watching him and waiting for something like that, his quickness still surprised her and if the Rohypnol hadn't slowed him down he would've grabbed her. He tried to get back to his knees, but that one effort was all he had left. Antoinette waited until she was sure that he was helpless, and then used a bed pillow to smother him.

She sat for a half hour after that to gather her wits, and then left the motel room and drove off in Lance's car. For the last two weeks she was convinced she was going to be killed, but the nightmare was finally over and she'd been given a second chance. She wasn't going to Montana, though. Fuck that! Los Angeles was her future. As she proved to Lance, she could be one hell of an actress when properly motivated.

ACKNOWLEDGMENTS

I'd like to thank Michael Bracken and Trey Barker for inviting me to contribute to this novella series. Trey was one of my guest editors when I ran my webzine Hardluck Stories, and I also had the privilege of publishing several of Trey's stories, so when asked, I was certainly going to return the favor.

GUNS+TACOS CREATED AND EDITED BY   MICHAEL BRACKEN & TREY R. BARKER

STACY WOODSON

TWO TAMALES, ONE TOKAREV, AND A LIFETIME OF BROKEN PROMISES

SEASON
3

GUNS+TACOS

EPISODE
14

TWO TAMALES, ONE TOKAREV, AND A LIFETIME OF BROKEN PROMISES

Stacy Woodson

A minister, a taco truck, and a gun. The setup sounds like the opening of a late-night comedy schtick—at least when Leno was still on the air. Back when a two-cent joke could get you a laugh. But the shit I'm dealing with isn't remotely funny.

It's the kind of thing that gets you a nickel in federal prison.

The wind blows, and it smells like I'm standing in front of some Taco Tuesday toilet bank waiting to take a leak, not standing in front of a food truck waiting to buy a burner.

You may be wondering why I'd risk my reputation, my life, to do this. Here's the thing, I wasn't always a clergywoman. And my brother Tommy—I'm the only hope he's got left.

I hang back while a couple of glassy-eyed, twenty-somethings, laughing too loud, stare at the menu. I look past them across the street at the tall high-rises—condos probably filled with young

53

yuppies who like artisanal cheeses and gourmet coffee and organic cotton sheets.

I wonder if East Side Edna sent me to the right place, if this truck is really legit.

At least there isn't a chance I'll be recognized in this high-end neighborhood. And would it really matter anyway?

If I am stopped, I'll flash my collar. A minister walking the streets of Chicago isn't something new. There are plenty of night ministers tending to the homeless and disaffected youth.

The couple still screw around at the window.

I continue to wait. My anxiety continues to build.

And I curse Tommy for putting me in this position again.

I plunge my hands into the front pocket of the hoodie, the one I borrowed from the church's lost and found, and watch a police cruiser drive by—lights on, no sirens, tires hissing against the wet pavement.

And my minister story suddenly doesn't feel so plausible anymore.

I imagine what it would be like to get pinched. To go back to prison. No fresh air. No open windows. The view of my world through a bean slot in a steel door.

I can nearly feel the silver bracelets on my wrists, the metal digging into my skin, smell the remnants of sweat and puke left by some drunk in the back seat of the police cruiser.

And I almost want to puke myself.

I fight the urge to sit, put my head between my legs. I'll be damned if I look like that puking pastor at the Lombardo Brothers Funeral Home. So, I yank down the zipper on the hoodie instead and hope the cool air will be enough.

The couple finally orders. They take their paper bags already pooled with grease and stumble across the street toward the condos.

It's finally my turn at the truck. I remember Edna's instructions.

Ask for Jessie, then the special.

I walk up, but no one is at the window. I look at the menu. No specials, and some of the selections are fancy—nearly gourmet—and my doubts about Edna's intel returns.

"What can I get you?" a velvet voice asks.

At the window there's someone with an Adam's apple the size of my fist and a face like a Maybelline ad.

My eyes go wide.

She narrows hers.

"You Jessie?" I ask, my tone meek, cautious.

She brings a cigarette to her lips. Her bicep strains against the sleeve of her leopard print shirt. She takes a long drag, seems to study me.

"Depends." She exhales the word. "Which Jessie you looking for?"

I frown, not expecting this.

"The one spelled with an E or the one with an I-E?" she asks.

I know this is some kind of test, a test I will likely fail, and I decide I'm not going to play her game. "The one that's spelled with a J."

She laughs. I can't tell if she accepts my answer, or if she's simply amused by it. I continue anyway. "I'd like the special."

More smoking, more staring—like she's still sizing me up. Until her eyes stop at my neck, and her face hardens.

I reach up, but even before I touch it, I know why she's alarmed. My hoodie is still unzipped. She's spotted my clerical collar. The white must look like some beacon under Chicago's hazy-orange street lights. I wonder if she's worried I'm 5-O, or the hand of God will strike her down if she helps me.

Either way I'm screwed.

Without the gun, I can't help Tommy. And without my help, he's dead.

She reaches for the handle on the concessions window like she's about to close it, drive away, and leave me standing at the curb.

My mind scrambles. I try to find an angle, a way to convince her to change her mind. But trust is a tricky thing, and I've got nothing to offer her.

"Viv?" A voice I know says my name.

I tense. So much for anonymity.

My mind goes back to the police cruiser, and vomit tickles my throat. I swallow hard and fight the urge to walk away. I need that gun.

Gianna emerges from the back of the truck. She looks the way I remember—red hair, wild eyes, a hooked nose like Gonzo-the-Muppet. When we parted ways, it wasn't exactly on good terms. I wonder if she still holds a grudge.

"Hooker, you know this fool?" Jessie asks Gianna, hand still poised to shut-down the truck.

Gianna pops her gum and stares at me just like Jessie did.

I wait to see how she's going to play it. This could work in my favor or seal my brother's fate.

"I know her," she finally says, her tone neutral.

Not exactly a ringing endorsement, but Jessie lets go of the window. "Didn't realize you found religion, G."

"It's not like that." Gianna works her gum again. "Viv was my cellie. We did time together."

Jessie raises two perfectly plucked eyebrows. From the look on her face it's clear she's heard about me, and what she's heard isn't good.

I forge ahead anyway. "I'm here for the special," I tell Gianna, hoping the vibe I'm getting is wrong. That despite everything, she will help me.

She and Jessie exchange a look—a look I don't understand. And I think they're going to tell me to go fuck myself.

But then Gianna's face brightens. "Dos tamales—deconstructed?"

Jessie smiles. "Fully loaded?"

Gianna nods.

"Coming right up."

I'm stunned, but I guess I shouldn't be. Gianna has always

been a business woman at heart.

Jessie grabs a Styrofoam food container, removes grit cakes from the warmer and tops them with pork, corn salsa, and sour cream. Then, she puts the container into a large paper bag and hands it to Gianna. When she disappears into the back of the truck, Salsa music starts to play.

Except for a brown sedan, engine running, the street is empty, and Gianna and I are alone. She tells me the price. I pull out the money I borrowed from Edna and give her the cash. She hands me the bag. Then, leans against the window.

"After I got out, I envied you, Viv—the way you turned your life around. Guess the more things change, the more they stay the same."

I tighten my grip on the bag, think about what's inside and everything that brought me here.

For once in her life Gianna's right, and the truth hurts almost as much as my brother's betrayal.

I guess this is the part where I tell you how this all started—how I got suckered into cosigning on my brother's problems, again.

It's complicated, really. But in the interest of time, I'll spare you *most* of the gory details.

It started when we were kids.

I know what you're thinking—this is the short version? But our childhood is important. It shaped the choices we made, and it's how I ended up here.

Tommy and I grew up in the foster care system, which is basically a gladiator academy for criminals. With more placements than birthdays, we were exposed to new kids, new "parents," new threats, and new lessons on how to steal, how to hustle, how to survive. On our fifteenth placement, the social worker tried to separate Tommy and me. Some bullshit about being unable to find a family who would take both of us.

We decided to run away and became two hustlers living on

the streets. We lived by a set of rules: #1 no drugs, #2 no turning tricks, #3 no tangling with the mob—and we'd have each other's back always. We refused to become our parents. After that, any way we could get scratch was fair game.

We worked the streets during the day, slept on the "L" at night. Sometimes, we even had enough money to rent one of those pink palace suites at the Rainbow motel or buy a ticket to the movies. Mobster flicks were our favorite. And the irony isn't lost on me now.

Eventually, we became adults. Moved from picking pockets and simple cons to bigger scores. We did this for years and had a good run until I got rolled-up for a B&E—a B&E committed by my brother.

Of course, I took the fall. I promised Tommy I'd have his back. And I'd never break my word. Without each other, we had nothing else.

During my stint in prison, I found religion, went straight. But Tommy, he's still hustling. At least he was until two days ago, when he walks into Divine Sinners—my church on the East Side of town.

It is the end of Sunday service, the beginning of Lent—my favorite time of year. Forty days of reflection, soul searching, and spiritual renewal. I'll spare you the rest of the religious mumbo jumbo except to say that when my brother Tommy enters the church, I think there's been some kind of Lenten miracle. That my prayers have finally been answered. Then, I see the look on his face—a look I've seen countless times before—and I know I need to keep praying.

He takes a seat in one of the pews, doesn't have the decency to remove his ballcap, while I walk to the vestibule and shake hands with my parishioners.

You may think it's odd that an ex-con, someone who is anti-establishment like me, is a minister. I'm not going to blow sunshine up your ass and say this church is somehow different. It's still organized religion and by definition a traditional institution. But it's organized religion on my terms—at least with as much leeway as the Bishop will give me.

I don't care if parishioners are Christian, atheist, or even if they're Packers fans. (Okay, maybe that's where I draw the line.) I still point them toward God. That's the job.

But this isn't the main reason my doors are open.

I want this church to be a safe place where people can be real and authentic, a place where they feel accepted. Somewhere they can turn when they're digging for hope. The kind of place I wish Tommy and I had when we were kids.

I continue to shake hands with ex-gangbangers, not-so-ex-gamblers, drug addicts, the ex-cons I met through my prison ministry, and other ordinary people from our East Side neighborhood. Some are friendly. Some won't look me in the eye. One admires the tattoo of Mary Magdalene on my forearm. I try to focus on each person, give them my full attention. But I'm distracted. My mind is on my brother.

I glance toward the sanctuary. The doors are propped open. My brother still sits in the pew. His bloodshot eyes stare back at me. I wonder what kind of trouble he's in this time. I decide it must be big.

Big enough to bring him here.

"You alright, Viv?" Edna asks.

She's last in line. I tower over her, which isn't hard to do when you are six-feet tall. You'd never guess she's a bookie by the way she looks—grandmotherly like that actress Betty White from *The Golden Girls*. The kind of person who likes to read mysteries and drink tea and owns a cat with some literary name like Edgar or Agatha or Sherlock. But the only tea Edna drinks is a Long Island, and the only pet she owns is a Pitbull named Reggie.

Guess you can't judge a bookie by her cover.

Besides running numbers, Edna is also a culinary queen who likes to feed me. She knows I can't cook. Even boiling water is a skill I don't possess. She hands me a foil-covered dish. "It's chicken pot pie. Crust is made from scratch, not frozen."

Her meals are the closest thing I've experienced to any kind of maternal affection, and my nerves go on edge. The foster-kid-in-me automatically looks for an angle—the food must be some bait and switch. I'll take the dish, and when my hands are occupied, she'll pull a Billie from her purse and club me for it—that kind of thing.

Because in the world where I used to live, kindness is always a prelude to pain.

But the adult-in-me knows this isn't true. There is no angle. Not from Edna. So, I take the dish and thank her for it.

I expect some kind of cooking instructions. That's what usually follows when she hands me something like this. But instead, she eyes Tommy through the open doors and steps closer to me, so close I can smell her Lucky Strikes and Jean Nate. "Watch out for that brother of yours," she whispers. "He's no good, Viv."

I think about our colorful congregation and laugh at the irony. "Come on, Edna. Are any of us good, really?"

The sweet expression on her face disappears. She grips my elbow, guides me toward the front door, her shoes click-clacking against the tile floor.

"You know what I do for a living. Been in the business a long time because I know when to keep my mouth shut. But I'll tell you this much. Your brother is sloppy and deep in the middle of something. If you're not careful, he'll pull you back in."

I've never seen this side of Edna, and it makes me uncomfortable. I ask if she's been watching *The Godfather* again and try to get a laugh.

But the look on her face doesn't waiver. "You're not far off the mark, kid."

She stares at me like she wants to make sure her words sink in.

And they do—like a body with concrete shoes dumped into Lake Michigan.

"Look, I like you," Edna says. "I like this church. You've

done something good here. Don't let your brother screw things up for you or the rest of us." She hikes her purse into the crook of her arm, and the smile on her face returns. "Three hundred and fifty degrees on that pot pie. Bake for fifteen minutes."

I glance down at the foil-covered dish in my hands, mind still reeling about Tommy. He wouldn't break rule #3. He wouldn't be that stupid. Would he?

"Fifteen minutes," Edna says, again. "Any longer and the pie will be dry." She narrows her eyes. "Don't let my pot pie get dry, Viv."

"I won't. Thanks, Edna."

She pats my hand. "Any time, dear."

She glances back at my brother and shakes her head before she slips on her prescription sunglasses and click-clacks through the front doors.

After she leaves, I don't go back to the sanctuary. I signal my brother to wait. Then, I take the stairs to the basement, which is the closest thing we have to a church hall. There's a small kitchen, an old couch, a few folding tables and chairs. Typically, we hold meetings here—not about bake sales or food drives or Christmas pageant planning. We host AA meetings, anger management sessions, resume writing and job interview seminars. Anything to help parishioners navigate society successfully. Some participate, and that's great. Others don't and that's fine. My job is to offer them options.

I put Edna's pot pie in the fridge, walk over to a rack that I share with our lost and found. I push a hoodie aside, hang up my vestments. I pick up a hat and hang it up, too. Then, I tidy up some pamphlets about my prison ministry while I silently pray that God gives me the strength to navigate this crap with my brother.

When I'm ready, I go back upstairs.

I find Tommy near the front doors of the church. The Metallica T-shirt he's wearing is wrinkled, and his jeans bag at the seat. He motions for me to join him outside.

I follow him through the doors, down the stairs, and onto the sidewalk. The concrete is cracked—broken like most things on this side of town. I sidestep a section and continue to trail behind him. He dips into an alley—the one that runs alongside the church. We have some privacy but can still see the dilapidated two-flats across the street.

He reaches into his jeans, pulls out a pack of cigarettes.

"You know those will kill you."

He ignores me. Lips one out, lights the tip, inhales. "The flats across the street remind me of our first foster place. You know, the one on the South Side?"

I nod. I don't think about the place as much as the circumstances that sent us there.

Our mother left to meet her dealer, and Tommy was hungry. So, I dug through our cockroach-filled pantry and found a box of Mac and Cheese. I was too young to read and tried to make it from the pictures on the box. That's how the fire started.

That's why the social worker came.

"They had that shitty dog—the chihuahua." Tommy glances at a scar from a bite on his wrist. "What the hell was his name?"

"Poco."

"That's right." He shakes his head. "I hated that dog."

I watch him smoke. Study his face. Think about how much he's changed since my time behind bars. At the beginning of my stint he promised he'd turn over a new leaf. He even went straight. Got a job on a city crew for the Department of Sewers. Made decent money—enough to rent an apartment. Then, he hooked up with Arlene, and that's when he stopped visiting me.

That's when he started hustling, again.

He continues to smoke, brings up more foster-care memories. And I wait while he works up the courage to tell me what's really on his mind.

Two cigarettes later he finally finds his balls. "I'm down to the felt, Viv."

"Felt?" I frown. The word throws me. "What felt?"

"Poker."

I narrow my eyes. "But you stopped gambling." At least that's what he's been telling me. How he cut the cord on high-stakes poker games. How he's working on that new leaf.

When he speaks again, the stutter starts, something I haven't heard since I got arrested nearly ten years ago, and I know whatever he's dealing with is bad.

"S-s-started that way," he says. "But then, Arlene found out about this game. Some hush-hush underground thing. Real money on the table. Did I tell you sh-sh-she's pregnant?"

"Jesus, Tommy." My eyes go wide. My brother can barely take care of himself. "You sure it's yours?"

"Of course, it's mine," he snaps. He turns away. I can tell he's pissed.

I put my hand on his shoulder. "Come-on, Tommy. I had to ask. Arlene isn't exactly a one-man-kind-of-woman."

He narrows his eyes at me, flicks his cigarette butt into the alley, lights another. Then, he looks toward the flats again and slides into another memory.

"Tommy."

He blinks.

"The poker game."

"Yeah…" He takes another drag before he winds up again. "You gotta understand, Viv. I think this is my chance. Win big. Move to the burbs. Get a small house in a nice neighborhood. Give this kid the kind of life we didn't have. You know?"

I can't tell if he's sincere or if he's bringing up all the foster-care-bullshit because he's trying to work me. Either way, my patience is wearing thin. "How much do you owe?"

He stares at his feet.

"Tommy."

"Twenty."

"Grand?" My voice goes up an octave.

He still doesn't meet my eyes, and I know there's more.

"Plus the juice."

"You got a juice loan?"

"I didn't have a choice. The game was mobbed up, Viv."

"Christ almighty, Tommy," I yell. "You always have a choice."

I close my eyes, suck in a breath, fight the urge to put my fist through his face.

"What happened to our rules?" I ask, when I'm calm again. "No drugs, no turning tricks." I lower my voice. "Don't get tangled up with the mob."

"I know, Viv. I know." He yanks off his hat, rakes a hand through his hair. "But the thing is, we aren't kids anymore."

"We never played childish games. We never had that luxury. Those rules kept us alive. They were about survival."

"That's not the worst of it." He looks at his feet again.

I brace myself for the rest.

"Paulie's calling the note."

I stare at him, too stunned to say anything else.

"I made a stupid mistake with the juice loan, Viv. It's my first and last time. Get me out of this jam, and I'll turn over a new leaf."

I shake my head. I'm tired of this cycle of bullshit—Tommy and his gambling debt, me cleaning up his mess, his promise that he'll turn over a new leaf.

That this will be the last time.

"Screw you and your leaf, Tommy." I yank the pack of cigarettes from his pocket, light one and smoke it myself.

I should turn him over to the cops. Let him get busted. Jail time would be the best thing for him—provided the mob doesn't get to him behind bars. But then, I think about the baby, and it cuts straight to my heart. Arlene is useless—just like our mother. Tommy is that kid's only fighting chance. "What kind of timeline did they give you?"

"Seventy-two hours. If I don't come up with the money—" He looks at me wide-eyed.

"I know how it works."

We stand there for a few minutes, both of us leaning against the building, while I try to come up with a plan—some Hail Mary play that will save my brother's ass.

"We could rob a bank," he finally says.

He can't be serious.

"A convenience store?"

"Shut up, Tommy."

I take another drag from my cigarette and start to pray, the same prayer I said in the basement only this time with expletives. I'm not some pious prick. I always keep it real with God. When my cigarette is gone, I know what to do.

"I'll talk to him."

"To Paulie...." Tommy stares at me like he isn't sure he heard me right.

"Why not?"

He laughs.

"Mobsters—they're religious. Maybe if he knows your sister is a minister, he'll come up with a reasonable payment plan."

"Mobsters are Catholic, Viv. Not Lutheran."

"You got any better ideas?"

He doesn't. He never does. He gives me Paulie's address. Then, he hugs me. I hug him back. He may be a dumbass, but he's still my brother.

I crush out my cigarette and watch him walk up the street. A brown sedan slides past. More traffic. Then the city bus.

Tommy jogs to the bus stop and barely reaches it in time. I watch him find his seat. When the bus pulls away, my mind goes back to Edna—her warning.

Looking back now, I wish I'd listened to her.

Turns out Paulie-the-loan-shark is also Paulie-the-body-broker—not the kind of body broker who sells body parts. He owns a funeral home just outside of Chinatown.

The building is old, brick, with faded green awnings. Inside, it smells like a whorehouse. Okay, I've never been inside a whorehouse, but it's how I expect one would smell—cheap scented candles, too much perfume, old dusty carpets. To the left is the casket showroom, to the right a reception area, and in the back is a chapel—at least that's what the sign says in the lobby.

I walk through the lobby past a table that has a vase filled with Stargazer lilies and a framed newspaper clipping with a headline that reads:

Lombardo Brothers Funeral Home
Three Generations Dealing in Death

I wonder if people see this as an endorsement or if they think it's creepy like I do.

I find Paulie in the casket showroom. I recognize his face from the picture in the puff-piece. He looks like your classic salesman—short, bald, polyester suit. He's trying to upsell an old woman on a casket with shiny wood inlay.

"You're early," he says, noticing my collar. "The chapel room is in the back. You can get ready there."

I tell him I'm not here to officiate a funeral, but I'm not sure he hears me. His focus is on the woman. She's crying now. He guides her over to an aqua velvet couch and hands her a box of tissue.

I want to tell her that the casket doesn't matter. We all decompose the same way. But I know cock-blocking Paulie's sale isn't the best way to start a negotiation.

So, I wait in the corner of the showroom and look at the displays—urns, memorial jewelry, remembrance videos, forever-missed websites, fancy vehicles for funeral processions. All creative ways to up-sale, up-charge.

To profit from grief.

A loud sob pulls me back to the couch. The woman is hunched over now, her face in her weathered hands. Paulie puts his arm around her shoulders. He glances at his watch, but she doesn't seem to notice, still absorbed in her grief. When she stops crying, Paulie convinces her to finance her husband's funeral. They fill out some paperwork. After he closes the deal, he waddles over to me. "Can I help you?"

"Is there a place where we can talk privately?"

He glances at his watch again. "I've got the Ryan funeral starting soon."

"It will only take a minute."

"Did someone die?"

"No—"

"Are you here to arrange a funeral?"

"No—"

"Are you here to purchase anything?"

"No—"

"Then, you need to make an appointment."

I fold my arms. "Let me get this straight. You have time for me if I'm here to buy something."

"But you're not." He walks away.

"Hey!" I call after him. But he keeps going. And I stand there, slack-jawed.

So much for my minister angle.

I can't even get the guy to talk to me, let alone negotiate a payment plan for my brother.

Normally, I'd come back, try another day. But I can't. Tommy is on the clock, and there's too much at stake. I walk after him.

Before I can reach him, a man from "Once and Flor-al" stumbles into the showroom and intercepts Paulie. The flower arrangement he's holding looks like a cover candidate for the next Stephen King novel—white carnations and violets shaped like a head with wooden antlers. There are eyes, too—red, glass, creepy. It's like Cujo mated with Bambi. I'm no floral-matter-expert, but even I know some bloom-related crime was committed here.

"Delivery for the Ryan funeral."

Paulie stares.

67

For a second, I forget why I'm here, and I stare, too.

The man shifts the weight of the arrangement, pulls out a wadded-up piece of paper. "I'm sure the order said Lombardo Brothers Funeral Home."

"This is the right place," Paulie says, finding his voice. He rips his eyes away and yells for someone named Anthony.

A few seconds later, a pimple-faced teenager appears. He looks like a miniature version of Paulie except with a full head of hair.

"Yeah, Pop?" The kid stares at the flowers.

"Take this man to the chapel room. And find a place for—" Paulie looks at the delivery man and waits.

We all do.

"The elk." The man's tone implies this should be obvious. "It's from the lodge. Mr. Ryan was a member."

"Of course," Paulie says like this makes sense. But there's nothing that makes sense about this little shop of horrors. "Anthony, find a place for the *elk* in the chapel room. A nice corner."

"In the back, Pop?"

Paulie nods.

After Anthony disappears with the delivery man, I try again with Paulie. "Five minutes. That's all I'm asking."

I think he's about to agree, but then voices flood the lobby: men in business suits and thick sunglasses, women wearing dresses and wide-brimmed hats. A reporter arrives, too. I can tell he's from the newspaper because he carries a steno pad and a messenger bag with the name of the paper stitched on the flap.

Paulie's focus is on them, particularly the reporter. He pushes a business card at me. "Make an appointment."

He moves toward the lobby.

I clench my hands. I tried to be discrete, speak to the guy in private. But now I've had enough. "I'm here about a juice loan." My voice is loud.

Paulie whips around.

I have his full attention and from the look on his face, I know this isn't the kind of attention I want.

"We didn't plan on serving *juice and scones* in the reception room." His voice is louder than mine—so loud that if anyone is listening, they will think they misunderstood what I said.

He flashes a nervous smile at the reporter who is looking at us now and quickly adds, "But don't worry, I'm sure we can accommodate your request."

Then, he bellows for his son again.

When the kid appears this time, he's holding an easel and a funeral print—a photograph of a man with salt-and-pepper hair, kind eyes, and a Hollywood smile. I assume it's for the funeral.

"Open the chapel room for Mrs. Ryan's early guests," Paulie tells Anthony. "The preacher should be here soon. I will be in the back. I don't want to be disturbed."

With his new marching orders, Anthony disappears, again.

And I'm left with Paulie—the mobster I've managed to piss off. The same man who will decide my brother's fate. I wonder if this can get any worse.

Paulie tells me to follow him.

I do, through a door to a hall lined with photographs from the Lombardo family business.

I wonder what I can possibly say now that will change Paulie's mind about calling Tommy's note. He doesn't seem to care about my status with God. So, the clergy angle I planned to use is a bust. And I don't think pretty-please-don't-hurt-my-brother is going to work either.

We turn another corner.

Pass another door.

It's quiet back here, so quiet I can hear Paulie breathing. My anxiety starts to build. Any minute we will be at his office.

And I still have nothing.

So, I reach back to my hustling days. Think about Paulie like he's a mark and work through how I would play him. Mob man, family man, businessman, narcissist—I cycle through the few things I know about him, consider different angles, how I can leverage each.

In the end, I decide to focus on his enthusiasm for business. I need to show Paulie keeping my brother alive benefits his bottom line. It's a simple argument. If my brother's dead, Paulie won't get paid. And wouldn't smaller payments be better than nothing at all?

Paulie opens a door.

I follow him inside, ready to make my pitch.

Then, he flicks on the lights.

No filing cabinets, no desks, no chairs to sit and work things out like two civilized people. Instead, stainless steel tables and cabinets. Shelves filled with jugs and hoses and scalpels and other instruments that could moonlight as torture devices.

There's a body, too, on one of the tables. It's covered, but it doesn't matter. The outline underneath the sheet is enough to make my heart jackhammer in my chest.

I look for another door, another hallway, some indication that the embalming room is simply a stop along the way.

But there's no outlet, no windows.

There's only the door.

And Paulie shuts it.

I look back at the body and think about how easy it would be to disappear my brother. Kill him here. Use the crematorium in the back to dispose of his body.

How easy it would be to disappear me.

Paulie brought me here to intimidate me.

And it's working.

"You have my attention." Paulie folds his arms, leans against the table—the one with the body. "You should know if you want a loan, this is not the way to approach me."

"I don't need a loan. I'm here about my brother, Tommy. He tells me he owes you money."

He frowns. "He never mentioned a sister." He seems to

study me. "Tattoos, hard eyes. You don't look like a preacher. Are you a cop?"

"What?" My eyes go wide. "God, no—"

"A snitch—"

"No."

"Lift your shirt."

"Seriously?"

"Lift your shirt, or this conversation is over."

I'm not sure if I'm more pissed that I'm intimidated by this asshole or that he thinks I'm a cop. I shake my head and tug up my shirt.

He has me turn so he can see my back.

"Satisfied?"

"Nice ink," he says.

I take that as a "yes." I face Paulie and fix my shirt. "So, my brother—"

"Owes twenty Gs plus the juice," Paulie finishes.

"I want to see the note."

He stares.

Clearly, this is not what he expects. And frankly, I don't know why I said it. Maybe it's because I'm still rattled or maybe it's because I want Paulie to know he isn't going to intimidate me. That I have some fight in me, too.

Paulie's eyes narrow. "You think you can come into my business and make demands?"

"I think you are a businessman who wants to get paid twenty grand."

"Twenty grand *plus the juice*," Paulie emphasizes again. "At least that's what he owes this time." He goes over to a cabinet, pulls out a laptop, places it on an empty table, and taps the keys.

This is good. Paulie is willing to show me the note. Despite our rocky start, he seems reasonable. Maybe we can work out a deal, and Tommy can put this one-time-dance-with-The-Outfit behind him. My confidence is starting to build.

Until I process what Paulie said.

"What do you mean what he owes this time?"

Paulie doesn't seem to hear me, his focus is still on the laptop. A few more taps to the keys. Then, he rotates the screen so it faces me.

At first glance, it looks like an application for a funeral loan. My brother's information is listed at the top—driver's license, date of birth, job and salary, current assets. At the bottom are estimated funeral costs with all the upcharges and upgrades. It even includes a white dove release, something I somehow missed in the casket showroom.

All for a relative that doesn't exist.

The total cost is twenty grand, plus interest.

"You mentioned other loans?" I press, still focused on my conversation with Tommy. And the bullshit story he gave me about how this is his first juice loan.

Paulie motions he wants to join me on my side of the table. At the computer, he opens another file, and then, another. More applications, more loans, same setup, different amounts. Tommy's name is on all of them.

"It seems like a lot of people have died in my family." I wonder how long Tommy has been borrowing money. Does this end with Paulie, or does he owe more people money, too?

Part of me wants to turn Tommy over to Paulie. Hell, I want to kill him myself. But then, I think about the baby and the lifelong promise I made to my brother. "How about a payment plan? That's a lot of cash. Money I'm sure you want returned. Tommy can't pay you back if he's dead."

Paulie pushes his laptop closed. "I don't want to see Tommy hurt. He usually finds a way to earn, but I'm not the one calling the note."

I frown. "I don't understand. You said Tommy owes you twenty grand."

"Plus the juice," Paulie adds.

"Jesus," I say, still pissed. "Isn't that implied by now?"

Paulie shrugs. "The details are important."

There's a knock at the door.

Paulie ignores it. "Look, I broker the loan, take the payments, earn a fee, but I don't finance the money."

"Who does?"

More knocking.

Paulie yells, "I said no interruptions."

"This can't wait, Pop."

Paulie sighs. Then, opens the door.

Anthony is standing there, face tight.

"What," Paulie says.

"Sorry, Pop. It's just..." He leans in and whispers something in his father's ear.

Paulie's eyes go wide. "I'm sorry," he tells me. "This thing with your brother is out of my hands."

Paulie and Anthony leave me in the embalming room staring at the covered corpse on the stainless-steel table.

I imagine my brother under that sheet.

And Rule # 3 echoes in my head.

I wonder how my brother could be so stupid.

I need to come up with another plan to get the money. Unfortunately, the options I have will likely land us both in prison.

Still, the alternative is better than that table.

I walk down the winding hall, angry about my brother's lies, frustrated because I don't know what to do, praying for some kind of epiphany.

And then, I get one—when I find Paulie and Anthony in the casket showroom standing in front of a drunk man.

He's sitting on the aqua velvet couch, head between his legs, humming "Amazing Grace." The way the man's dressed, I assume he's the officiant for the Ryan funeral.

"What's wrong with him?" Paulie asks.

"He's drunk," Anthony says. "Vodka. Came from a Russian wedding—at least that's what I think he said."

Still humming, the man tries to sit up.

Fails.

Paulie glances at the lobby which now looks like an AARP ad—elderly men in blue suits, some with walkers or canes, others in wheelchairs. Many wear medals or pins that look like Cujo's spawn.

"Has anyone seen him?" Paulie asks.

"I'm not sure," Anthony whispers. "It gets worse, Pop. Someone from the paper is here."

"I know." Paulie rubs the back of his neck.

"This could look really bad for us."

"How much time do we have?"

"Ten minutes, if we want to start on time."

"Give him some coffee."

"I've already tried."

Paulie mutters something in Italian that I'm sure isn't G-rated.

"I'm fine," the man slurs. He tries to sit-up again. His face turns red, his hand goes to his mouth.

I reach for an empty urn—one from a display—and thrust it toward him.

He retches inside.

Paulie and Anthony look like they are about to retch, too. Anthony from the smell, and Paulie from the cost of the urn the man just ruined.

If Paulie is surprised I'm still here, he doesn't show it. He's too focused on the puking pastor and the people milling in the lobby.

"You're going to have to officiate the service, Pop."

Paulie shakes his head. "Mrs. Ryan was clear. She wants a member of the clergy not a funeral director."

"I don't think we have a choice."

This is when the epiphany I mentioned hits me. I know how to leverage this situation to work for Tommy and for me.

"It's a shame," I say to Paulie. "So many aging lodge members here. So many future business opportunities. Too bad there isn't a minister here who can help."

I walk toward the front door. Then I hear the pastor retch again. And I couldn't have timed it better.

"Wait," Paulie calls.

I suppress a smile before I face him again.

"Officiate the funeral, and I'll put you in touch with my boss."

I look at the crowd in the lobby to remind Paulie the business he stands to lose. "I want a payment plan for my brother."

"It's like I told you before, it's not my decision. You want a payment plan for Tommy. I can put you in touch with the guy calling the note. This is the best I can do."

It's not what I want. But I agree to his terms.

It's not like I have another choice.

A few minutes later, I'm in the chapel room. It's a conservative group. On one side of the room are people dressed like they are going to Buckingham Palace and on the other are people dressed like they are going to a lodge convention. The weird in here doesn't match my congregation, but it's still weird in its own way.

Paulie and Anthony stand in the back.

Mr. Ryan's casket is closed and in front of the room. It's flanked by his funeral print and that god-awful flower arrangement. So much for Anthony finding a nice corner in the back.

When I take my place at the lectern, I feel like everyone is gawking at me, including the elk. With my spiked hair and colorful tattoos, I'm sure I'm the last person they expect to see officiating. But in the end, it doesn't matter. I just need to get through this and keep my deal with Paulie.

The service lasts about forty-five minutes. I give people an opportunity to speak. Then, I go through some readings and prayers. Unfortunately, the eulogy isn't as personal as I would like it to be. I don't know anything about Mr. Ryan or the lodge and its members. But I know about community, the one I built at my church. And I talk about finding something special like this—a place where people are accepted and welcome. How the lodge plays this role in lives like Mr. Ryan's.

When the funeral concludes, I guess I did something right because Mrs. Ryan, teary-eyed, thanks me. The reporter approaches me, too. That's when I learn Mr. Ryan was responsible for spearheading several community-outreach programs, and this is the reason for the news coverage. I'm sorry I didn't know him because he sounds like my kind of guy.

When we are done chatting, the reporter says something to Mrs. Ryan about scones in the reception room. I don't have the heart to tell them that they will be disappointed.

When the room finally empties, I join Paulie.

"Not bad," Paulie says. "I had my doubts at first—"

"Spare me the nicey-nice. I held up my end of the bargain. Now, I expect you to hold up yours."

"I'll put you in touch with my boss."

"That wasn't our deal."

"That *was* our deal."

"I want contact information. I want to know where I can find him."

"You don't find Nick-the-Noodle. Nick-the-Noodle finds you."

I hope Nick-the-Noodle has some sense of urgency and meets with me before he decides to roll up my brother.

When I get back to the church, I empty my pockets, and notice my cell phone has missed calls from Tommy. I consider calling him back, but I'm still pissed about Paulie's revelation—that my brother has been riding the wave of gambling loans for years. I know it won't be a civilized conversation, and I'm not in the mood to get into it with him.

Still, I call him anyway.

But he doesn't answer his phone.

With nothing left to do but wait, I retreat to the basement, heat up Edna's pot pie, grab my cell phone again and scroll through the local news. It looks like the newspaper already posted the funeral piece: *Ryan Funeral—prison minister talks about the power of community and acceptance.*

I cringe. Not about the article. About the headline.

I wonder how Mrs. Ryan feels about it, how it will bode for Paulie's business, why I even care.

I try my brother, again.

No luck.

An hour later, I'm halfway through the pie when I hear footsteps upstairs.

This isn't unusual. I leave the side door to the church unlocked for my parishioners, and I'm not alarmed. Until an Andre the Giant lookalike comes down the stairs.

When he ducks to clear the ceiling, I push back from the folding table and grab the knife I used to cut the pie.

You may think it's weird that this is my first reaction: to go for the knife. But I grew up on the streets. And that whole thou shalt not kill thing...

Religion is a study in ambiguity.

I believe thou shalt not kill means thou shalt not murder, and I have no problem defending myself.

"Nick wants to see you."

Andre's voice is high-pitched like a kid going through puberty. If the circumstances were different, I may have been surprised, but right now I am still in fight or flight mode.

I leave the knife, tell Andre to give me a minute while I cover up Edna's pot pie, put it in the fridge, and recover from the adrenaline dump.

Part of me is relieved that this is my chance to talk to Nick and make things right. But I'm also uneasy. My brother's future rides on this meeting, and I don't know what I'm walking into. "Where are you taking me?" I ask—only an idiot wouldn't.

He folds his arms which are as wide as my thighs. "You'll see when we get there."

My gut tells me to hide the knife and take it with me. My eyes go back to the table, but Andre must have moved it because the knife is no longer there.

So, I reach for my phone.

"No phones."

I narrow my eyes. And we both stare at each other like two kids daring the other to blink. I try to read him, get some idea what's about to happen. But he gives me nothing. The man has no micro-expressions, and it's frustrating as hell.

I return my phone to the table, and Andre pats me down, which is almost as humiliating as my encounter with Paulie. When the grope-fest is over, we walk upstairs through the church and out the front door.

I'd love to say there are cameras mounted on one of the buildings along the street. That if something happens to me, the cops can do the whole CSI thing and find my body.

But there are no cameras in this neighborhood.

Andre stops next to a black Cadillac Escalade. The windows are dark, tinted. He opens the door to the backseat, and part of me expects to see Nick there.

But the seat is empty.

"Get in," Andre says.

I stare at the seat. The leather is clean and shiny, like the SUV is newly detailed. And I wonder how many people have survived after they've climbed inside.

I swallow, debate whether or not to leave.

If I go, they *may* kill me. If I don't go, they *will* kill Tommy.

And then, there's the baby.

I have no choice.

I climb inside.

From the outside, Salerno's looks like one of those ma-and-pa joints. You know the kind of place where everyone knows your name—unless a stranger asks.

Then, no one knows who the hell you are.

The sign in the window says the restaurant is closed, but Andre opens the door anyway.

Inside, the space is small. The ceilings are low. The walls are lined with racks filled with wine and pictures that look like headshots from a Scorsese film. A handful of café tables with red-checkered tablecloths fill the floor. All are empty except for one against the back wall. A man in velour sweats sits alone. He's a slight man, thin. I wonder if his nickname is because he likes pasta or if it's tied to something sinister.

I approach the table. He's scrolling through his phone. On the screen is the story about the Ryan funeral.

"Thanks for meeting with me," I tell him.

"You did good by Paulie." He taps his phone. "This—I appreciate."

I hope this will buy my brother some goodwill, and Nick seems pleasant enough. But I know how quickly things can change.

"I see you've met my head of security." Nick nods toward Andre, who is standing like a sentry, arms folded, at the front door. Then, he points to an empty chair.

If I sit where he wants, my back will be toward The Giant. If this goes bad, I want to see it coming. I want a fighting chance. So, I choose another chair.

This doesn't seem to bother Nick.

"I understand my brother owes you money."

Nick waves my comment away. "Food first. Then, business."

"There's no need. I just ate."

He ignores me, snaps his fingers, and a waiter scurries over.

"Two plates of spaghetti aglio eo olio. And a bottle Chianti."

"I'm fine with water."

Nick frowns. "Why? Are you one of those preachers who

doesn't drink?"

"No."

"Good," Nick says. "I don't trust teetotalers."

And I don't trust mobsters.

But of course, I don't say this. I'm not stupid.

Nick dismisses the waiter, and the man heads toward the kitchen.

"Wait until you taste the food." Nick kisses his fingertips and tosses them into the air. "Authentic. Like my Nona used to make. God rest her soul."

Normally, I would enjoy the culinary lesson. Even family histories intrigue me. But the only family I care about right now is my brother.

"About Tommy—"

Nick shakes his head. "Food first."

I sigh inwardly. If I can't discuss business, what am I supposed to do? Sit in silence? Make small talk? What's considered casual conversation with a mobster?

How's the gambling business?

What's the going rate on a juice loan?

Are you related to Al Capone?

Thankfully, we only sit like this for a few minutes before our food arrives. It's enough to feed a family of eight.

The waiter pulls the cork on the Chianti, pours two glasses, leaves the bottle.

I grab my glass and take a sip.

Nick makes the sign of the cross, clears his throat, and stares at me expectantly.

It takes me a second, but then I get it. He wants me to bless the food.

The smart ass in me wants to say something cheeky like rub-a-dub-dub-thanks-for-the grub—a fitting prayer for this dinner party farce. But I don't have the upper hand. So, I stick with a traditional Catholic prayer.

When I'm done, Nick makes the sign of the cross again,

straightens in his seat, and points to my plate. "Mangia."

He waits while I wind the pasta around my fork and take a bite. He asks if I like the food. I tell him it's delicious. And it's true. But I would have said it anyway.

Like I said earlier, I'm not stupid.

He focuses on his food. I nibble at mine. Halfway through the meal he lifts a checkered napkin, wipes his mouth, and says, "Tell me about you."

I straighten in my seat, hope this is the moment when we finally get down to business. "I'm here about Tommy's debt."

He shakes his head. "Not *why* you're here. I want to know more about you."

He can't be serious.

I can't imagine this guy gives two shits about my life or my ministry or my crappy childhood. Suddenly, I feel like I've been thrown into a game, and I don't know the rules.

"How is that relevant?"

"Call me old fashion but I like to know who I'm doing business with," Nick says.

"Tommy owes you money. He wants to pay you back. I'll make sure he's good for it. These are the details you need to know." I try to keep the edge out of my voice, but just mentioning Tommy's gambling debt makes me pissed, again.

Nick frowns. I can tell by the way he stares, he doesn't like what I said or maybe it's just the way I said it.

My stomach tightens.

Rule #3 echoes in my head like some public safety announcement.

Every instinct tells me to push back from the table, make a run for the kitchen, find the back door. All the snatch-and-grabs Tommy and I did when we were kids, I'm good at judging distance. And I'm confident I can get there before Nick can reach me—even Andre.

But then, I realize if I'm lucky enough to make it to the street, nothing has changed. Tommy is still a dead man walking unless I can alter his fate.

So, I remain at the table, fold my arms, try to project some kind of strength.

Try to forget that one word from Nick and Andre will rip me in two.

"I'm not sure what you want to hear," I finally say. "My childhood wasn't the best. But letting your past define you is a weak excuse not to make something of yourself. It took a stint in prison for me to realize life is about choices. I've made good ones and bad ones—and I own those."

"Then why don't you let your brother own his?"

He waits.

I shift in my seat.

He expects an answer.

When did Nick-the-Noodle become Nick-the-Shrink?

The waiter refills our wine and whisks away our plates.

And Nick still waits.

"Because I made him a promise," I finally say.

Nick nods like he gets this. "Promises to family are a sacred thing."

I think we're done. But we're not. He asks more questions—this time about my prison ministry, my stint. And I answer.

What else am I going to do?

I can't lie. Not because I'm pious. Nick's bullshit meter is more sensitive than mine. If I don't tell him the truth, he'll continue to probe. And despite all the back and forth, I still can't figure out his angle.

Frustrated, I ask, "Are we going to talk business, or am I just dinner entertainment?"

Nick narrows his eyes. But he doesn't answer because his cell phone rings.

He lifts it to his ear. "Is it done?"

I think about Tommy and wonder if this is connected to my brother.

I lean forward, stare at Nick, try to read his face. But just like Andre, he gives me nothing.

He ends the call, tugs the napkin from his collar, wipes his mouth, and tosses it onto the table. When he looks at me this time, I know something has changed. "Paulie told me you want to negotiate a payment plan for Tommy."

I nod.

"I immigrated to the States as an infant. Grew-up in Oak Park in a two-flat with three generations of my family. They are my blood, and I would do anything for them. Tommy is your brother, your family. This—I respect."

I think he's about to give Tommy a break, agree to my plan. That this bizarre-touchy-feely-trip-down-nightmare lane was worth it because this will be over.

Until he folds his arms and says, "The answer is no."

My mind trips on the word. "No?"

"No," Nick says.

But this doesn't make sense. He agrees family is important. He's a businessman. His life is about making money. I make my argument, the same one I made to Paulie.

"It's not about the money," Nick says.

"It's always about the money."

"Not this time."

So, I make another argument. This time, I go for the religious angle. Try to leverage the Catholic culture of forgiveness. I remind him that murdering my brother is a mortal sin.

Nick nods. He's listening. But the expression on his face remains the same. "There's a difference between crime and sin," he says. "Killing is a sin Christ understands and forgives in the name of business. Heaven is full of Made Men."

It's like I said earlier—religion is a study in ambiguity. In some twisted way Nick may be right. And I don't know where to go from here.

"If it's not about the money, there must be another way my brother can make restitution."

"There isn't," Nick says. "But you can."

"Me?" I stare at Nick not sure I heard him right. "I'm a minister. I took a vow of poverty."

"Like I said, it's not about the money."

"Then, I can't imagine how I could possibly—"

"Let's just say you have a unique set of verifiable skills."

I narrow my eyes. "As a thief or a minister?"

"Both."

Then, I finally see it—Nick's angle.

I didn't orchestrate this meeting. He did. He knew my background, my life, the kind of relationship I had with my brother before I even got here. He called the note on Tommy's debt early.

Not because he needed the money.

He knew my brother would come to me for help. That I would want to protect him. He used my brother to get to me.

This was his play all along.

The street kid in me admires his ingenuity. But the adult in me is pissed. Pissed because I should have seen it coming. Pissed because I wouldn't be in this position if Tommy had followed our rules.

This still leaves me wondering if Paulie was in on it too. And if Nick knew all this before I came, why all the chitchat during dinner? Why the pretense?

"What do you want me to do?" I ask.

He tells me he wants me to go to the prison, meet with a former associate of his father's. "Carmelo is only allowed to meet with the warden and his spiritual advisor," Nick explains. "That's where you come in."

I don't even know the job, and I can already see problems with Nick using me as his access and placement plan. The most obvious being the whole Catholic thing.

What Catholic would meet with a spiritual advisor that isn't a priest?

Of course, that's assuming Carmelo is actually a Catholic.

"You want me to give him a message?" I ask, looking for some clarity. "Smuggle something inside?"

Nick shakes his head. "I want you to smuggle something out."

I frown. I don't get it. Everyone knows the jail is mobbed up. Hell, I even saw it during my stint. Guards took bribes to smuggle in cell phones, drugs, cigarettes.

To look the other way.

"Why me?" I ask. "Why not buy access? Isn't that what you would normally do?"

"It's not that simple. Carmelo is in solitary. This kind of thing is delicate and can't be trusted with just anyone."

Then, Nick tells me a story about a mob hit. How Carmelo murdered Nick's father when he was a kid. That they never found the body.

"Of course, I want to avenge my father's death. That's my responsibility as his son. But my mother made me promise before I kill Carmelo that I make him tell me the location of the body. So, my father can be buried in a Catholic cemetery with her on consecrated ground."

"Because people who are buried together in life are kept together in death." At least that's what I think he's getting at.

He nods. "Carmelo was arrested when I was still a kid and has been hanging onto this information as an insurance policy. I've been waiting for my moment—my chance to keep the promise I made to my mother. Carmelo is getting up in years. And my mother—" Nick's voice turns thick, "—fucking cancer."

I nearly feel bad for the guy until I remind myself that he played me. That one word from Nick and my brother's life is over.

"What makes you think Carmelo will give up the body?"

"Let's just say he and I have come to an understanding."

"That doesn't mean he'll tell me."

"He won't tell you the information. He'll give it to you." Nick reaches into his pocket and places a trifold on the table. On the cover is Saint Anthony—the patron saint of lost things.

Ironic because that's how I feel right now.

"Tomorrow morning you will get a call from the prison.

Father Kelly will be out sick. Carmelo will want spiritual counseling. They will request you. Slide the Saint Anthony trifold into your Bible and pass it to Carmelo through the bean slot in his cell door. He will replace the trifold with an identical one. Inside, it will have the information I need."

I'm still suspicious. It seems too simple. Sure, it's not uncommon to pass religious materials to prisoners. But if I get caught....

"My mother's dying. Could be any day. You do this for me—we both keep the promises we made to our families. You don't—" he shrugs, "—we both will be planning funerals."

I leave the restaurant with Andre. It's late. I'm guessing eleven p.m. I would check, but my phone is back at the church.

Outside, the street is nearly empty. But this time I'm not anxious about riding with The Giant. Right now, I'm worth more to Nick alive than dead.

On the drive, I start to question Nick's story about Carmelo—whether or not it's legit. He seemed sincere. But then again, most people do when they're angling for something they want.

I reach up, click on the dome light, open the trifold, run my hand along the seams. There's nothing raised, nothing unusual, nothing that will get me stopped when I go through prison security. I wonder if there is something special about it. Or if it's simply a signaling device from Nick.

I put the trifold aside, turn off the light, and think about what he wants me to do.

I imagine getting caught again, going back to jail—the small walls, the isolation. There's my brother, too. If I fail, he will be a permanent resident of Lake Michigan.

And it's too much—even for me.

My chest goes tight.

I can barely breathe.

I grope for the door, roll down the window, suck in a breath. Then another—in-out-in.

I go on like this until my breathing finally steadies.

I lean back in my seat. Run through Nick's plan again. Even if I execute it successfully, there are no guarantees when Nick gets what he wants that he won't kill us both.

And then, there's the baby...

Screw this.

It's not worth the risk. There's too much to lose.

Tommy needs to take Arlene and go into hiding.

My minister network can help. We protect human trafficking victims, victims of abuse. But then I realize this is a bad idea. When Tommy disappears, Nick will suspect I'm helping him. And this will be the first place he looks.

Which leaves my brother with only one option—

He needs to go to the Feds.

Offer inside information on Nick's juice business, his illegal gambling ring, in exchange for WITSEC—not only for him but for Arlene and the baby.

I hate cops almost as much as I hate snitches. But this is about survival. And Tommy's chances are better with the government than they are with me.

Andre rolls up my window from the driver's seat, and it startles me. Then, I notice the dilapidated buildings, the busted-out streetlights outside, and I realize we are in my neighborhood.

He dumps me off in front of the church.

I make my way to the basement to find my phone so I can tell Tommy that he needs to go to the Feds. There are more missed calls.

All from Tommy.

There's a voicemail, too. I play the message.

"Where the hell are you, Viv? I need to know what happened with Paulie." The sound of cellophane. The flick of a lighter. I hear Tommy exhale. "I know this is going to sound weird, but I think someone is tailing me." He takes another drag from his cigarette, exhales again. Seconds pass, like he's thinking. "It's probably nothing. Just anxiety. Wish you'd answer your phone." He pauses. Another drag. "Came up with some scratch. Not much. A few hundred bucks. Good faith money for Paulie. That is—if your meeting went well. Call me when you—"

Then, silence.

I glance at the screen. Check there isn't some technological glitch. But the voicemail is over. Then, I get one of those sinking feelings—the kind you get when you watch a horror movie, and there's that classic trip-and-fall scene. You know what's going to happen, what's coming next. Still, you watch, wait, hope you're wrong.

I FaceTime Tommy.

The phone rings—the intergalactic sound whirls and whirls along with my anxiety.

I wait, hope I'm wrong. Even though, like the horror movie, I know what's coming next.

Nick's face fills the screen.

"I knew you'd call. Hey, Tommy, it's your sister."

The camera swings up, pans past cartons of tomatoes, a wall of spices, a commercial stove. "I'm sorry you didn't have a chance to talk to each other before you left," Nick continues while he takes me on a dizzying ride through Salerno's kitchen.

"Don't be rude, Tommy," Nick says. "Say hi to your sister."

He turns the camera. It's now on Tommy. He's tied to a chair—face beaten, eyes swollen shut. "I'm sorry, Viv," my brother whispers.

"I swear to god, Nick. You need to let him go or I will—"

"You'll what?"

Nick is right. What am I going to do? There's no chance Tommy can go to the Feds now. I wonder how long they've had him, when they brought him to Salerno's.

And then it hits me.

All the chit-chat with Nick—that dinner party farce. He was stalling, keeping me at the restaurant until they rolled up my brother.

It seems Carmelo isn't the only one who believes in insurance policies.

Nick's face is back on the screen. "Don't worry, you two will have an opportunity to catch up after you bring me what I want. I'll be in touch."

He ends the call.

And Rule #3 echoes in my head.

Fifteen minutes later Edna's with me in the basement at the church. So is her Pitbull, Reggie. She wears a yellow track suit, her purse slung in the crook of her arm. She looks feminine, delicate—a sharp contrast to her muscle-bound dog.

"Sorry for the late call," I tell her.

She waves my comment away. "Stanley Cup playoffs started tonight." She winks. "Reggie and I were still up." She lets Reggie off his leash, and he bounds toward me—jumps. Knocks me over and tries to lick me into submission.

Edna gives him the command to heel, and the dog immediately obeys. I scratch behind his ears while I tell Edna everything—how they have Tommy, how I'm in over my head. She doesn't say I told you so. Or I warned you. She nods, listens. That's the thing about Edna, she doesn't judge.

"Do you believe that sob story about Nick's mother?"

"Does it matter?"

"I guess it doesn't." She reaches for Reggie, rubs his ears, works her way down his neck. When she looks up, the expression on her face matches the one she had when she warned me about my brother. "You can still walk away from this."

"Yeah, right." I laugh.

"I'm serious, Viv. This is your brother's problem. Not yours."

"I made him a promise."

"How about the promises he made you?"

I think about my stint in prison. How I took the fall for Tommy so he could start over, take a new path, have a better life. How he broke that promise.

How he betrayed me.

"One thing my business has taught me is self-preservation," Edna continues. "Maybe it's time you consider yours."

She may be right. But despite everything, I can't turn my back on Tommy. I can't live in a world without him in it. "I won't abandon him, Edna."

The way she looks at me now I feel like she's already mourning my death. "You know, if you execute this plan the way Nick wants, when it's over, you and Tommy are loose ends. There's nothing stopping him from killing you both."

She's right. I've lived in Chicago my whole life and seen the mob's destruction, witnessed the carnage. It was the reason I made Rule #3. There are no happy endings with the mob. "I have to try, Edna. If I don't, I won't be able to live with myself."

We both stand there in silence. It's awkward now. I shouldn't have called and gotten her mixed her up in this mess. But I had nowhere else to turn.

The heater in the church clunks on, and a rush of air comes through the vent. Edna glances at the stairs, and I think she's going to leave. But instead, she says, "Do you have any coffee?"

"Instant."

"Well, don't just stand there. Pull it out. We're going to need it, if you want me to help you come up with a plan."

"I was hoping you'd say that."

"And, Viv..."

"Yeah?"

"Instant coffee." Edna shakes her head. "Haven't I taught you better than that?"

This brings me back to the taco truck—and the gun.

I'm on foot, nearly a block away, and Jessie's salsa music is finally starting to fade. I hug the bag of tamales to my chest, and the way the contents shift inside, it sounds like I've yanked open a junk drawer.

I wonder what Gianna gave me.

I fight the urge to look inside. That sedan, engine still running, is parked up the street. I worry it's one of Nick's goons. That they followed me just like they followed my brother.

So, I decide to wait and open the bag when I'm back at the church with Edna.

Once we started, it took an hour to come up with a plan—a way to turn the tables on Nick and save my brother's ass.

I will meet with Carmelo. Secure the information. Give it to Edna—there's no way I'm taking the only leverage I have and just handing it over to Nick. Once I negotiate Tommy's release, I will signal Edna, and she will text Carmelo's information to Tommy's cell phone.

And of course, there's the gun.

I'll bring it to the meet. I can't go unarmed. After Nick gets what he wants, it's the only thing I have to stop him from killing us both.

The plan sounds simple, but it's complicated, really.

As Nick's head of security, Andre will be there. He will pat-me-down—check for weapons, a wire, anything that will be a threat to Nick. It's not like I can show-up with the gun tucked into my waistband.

So, I devised a way to get the gun past The Giant.

Edna's job is to work the details.

At the church, I find her still in the basement with Reggie.

On a folding table are two Saint Anthony trifolds—the one from Nick and a copy I had Edna make. Also, there are two matching Bibles both liberated from the church. There's a carton of coffee and pastries, too.

Leave it to Edna to find something open this early in the morning.

I put the bag from the taco truck on the table.

"Garlic—" Edna wrinkles her nose. "I'm not a fan."

Tonight, neither am I. The smell takes me back to Salerno's, my meeting with Nick and everything that's brought me here.

"Did you take care of it?" I ask.

"Just like carving a turkey." Edna smiles. "Want to see it?"

I nod.

She opens the first Bible—the one I will bring to the prison. It's normal, the pages fully intact. Then, she opens the second Bible—the one I'll bring to the meet. It's hollowed out, the pages cut in the shape of a pistol.

"I hope it fits," Edna says.

I shrug out of the hoodie, toss it toward the Lost and Found rack. Then, unroll the bag, pull out the tamales, and peer inside. "Son-of-a—"

"What's wrong?" Edna asks.

"Gianna." I shake my head. "I never liked that bitch."

I tell Edna about my trip to the truck, my encounter with my former cellie—the grudge.

"This is the special—tamales *deconstructed*." And it's fully loaded—a fully loaded, steaming pile of shit.

I turn the bag over. And what falls out looks like tinker toys for convicts. I stare at the pieces, watch the barrel roll from the table and tumble onto the floor.

"You're going to need that," Edna says.

"You're assuming I know how to put it together."

"It's a Tokarev. It's just field stripped."

She says this like these details make a difference. But they mean nothing to me. Just because I lived on the streets and know how to use a gun, doesn't mean I know how to assemble one. Which makes me wonder why Edna knows so much about pistols and what else I don't know about her.

I start to ask, but Reggie whines.

Caught up in the gun debacle, I nearly forget he's there.

"He needs to go out." Edna hands me his leash. "Do you mind? When you come back I'll have the gun assembled." She starts to organize the pieces.

I call to Reggie and wait while he lumbers up the stairs.

Outside, the temperature dropped like it usually does before sunrise.

I always hate this time of day.

It reminds me of prison. The first call, the one right before headcount. When they flip on the lights, and I am jarred awake—the first reminder I am still behind bars.

I walk past Edna's powder-blue Oldsmobile. It's parked in the loading zone for the city bus. There's a handicap placard on the dash. I shake my head. She's one of the fittest people I know. Leave it to Edna to work all the angles.

Reggie finds a streetlamp already corroded by urine and lifts his leg.

While I wait for him to finish, I watch a homeless man turn the corner pushing a shopping cart. He struggles with the wheels against the uneven pavement. I loop Reggie's leash around the streetlamp and walk over to help.

As I get closer, he tries to back up and wheel away, but the shopping cart slams into the sidewalk so hard that it knocks the porkpie hat off his head. He has a buzz cut. It looks fresh. He must be new to this gig.

There are so many homeless veterans these days.

I wish I had time to talk so I could tell him life gets better than this. But all I can do is hand him his hat, help him with the cart, and slip him a few dollars.

I return to the basement with Reggie.

Just like Edna promised, the gun is assembled. I pick up the gun, pull back the slide, and a round cycles into the chamber. I place the pistol inside the Bible, along with the decoy pamphlet, and close the cover. Then, I lift both books.

The one with the gun feels different, weighty.

"I think we're set," Edna says.

I stare at the books, think about all the ways this can go wrong. "What are the odds we pull this off?"

Edna shrugs.

You know things are bad when even a bookie won't give you the odds.

* * *

I am asleep in the basement when I get the call from the prison.

Edna's racked out, too.

The conversation goes the way Nick told me it would—Father Kelly is out sick, and an inmate needs spiritual counseling.

When I end the call, Edna sits up on the couch and swings her legs to the floor, nearly colliding with Reggie.

"Things are in motion." I tell her.

"When is the prison expecting you?" she asks, her voice still foggy from sleep.

"An hour."

Edna stands, walks over to the table, shakes the carton of coffee, pours what's left into a cup and heats it in the microwave. "Any word about the exchange from Nick?"

"Not yet."

"I've been thinking about the meet."

So have I. How Tommy's life depends on the outcome. How mine does, too.

"I think Reggie and I should take you to the prison. When you finish with Carmelo, we can swap the Bibles in the car."

I consider her suggestion. Nick's unpredictable. Once I have the information he wants, who knows when he will send Andre for me. I agree this is the best play.

"Now that's settled, you should change. Don't you think?"

I look down at my pants, my shirt, touch my clerical collar—the same outfit I've worn for two days, and it shows.

"Today, should be business as usual, Viv," Edna presses. "Just another visit as part of your prison ministry. Confidence matters. If you go there looking like that, smelling like that—" she waves a hand in front of her nose. "You'll draw attention to yourself—attention you don't want."

Edna's right. If I weren't so spun-up, I would have realized this myself. I go to the rack where I keep my vestments, fish out some fresh clothes.

When I'm done changing, Edna drains her coffee and hands me both Bibles. "You have a plan, Viv—a plan that may actually work. You can do this."

God bless her. I'm not sure if she believes it, or she's just being supportive.

Still, Edna's pep talk has its intended effect. It reminds me that things aren't over yet.

That there's still hope.

Then, my cell phone rings. I see Tommy's name. And all that hope disappears.

I accept the call, press speaker so Edna can hear.

"It's a great day, don't you think?" Nick says.

"I got the call about Carmelo." I cut to the chase. I'm in no mood for Nick's twisted version of pleasantries.

"This—I know."

"I want to talk to Tommy."

"When the job is done."

Suddenly, I worry the beating Nick's goons gave Tommy was too much. That he's already dead. "No brother. No job."

Nick says nothing.

And I'm afraid I'm right. I open my mouth to demand answers. But Edna stops me.

So, I stare at the phone and wait, the silence nearly killing me.

Finally, Nick sighs. Then, footsteps. Something rips. An audible wince.

I pull the phone closer and whisper, "Tommy?"

He sucks in a ragged breath.

"Jesus, Tommy, are you, okay?"

"I...n-n-n," A long pause. A breathy exhale. "I n-n-n-eed a smoke."

I laugh.

"You think I'm kidding?"

"You know those will kill you."

"That's the least of my problems right now, don't you think?" He laughs. Then, groans in pain.

My eyes go to the Bible—the one with the Tokarev. I think about the meet with Nick. How good it will feel to finally have the upper hand and turn the tables on that prick.

"You've talked to your brother." Nick is on the phone, again. "Now it's time to talk business."

"I'm listening."

"Tell me the plan. The details are important."

I go over what he expects. How I'm going to pass the Bible with the Saint Anthony trifold to Carmelo, how Carmelo will replace it with an identical trifold that has Nick's information inside.

"That's good. There's just one more thing…"

I frown, replay the conversation from Salerno's in my head, and I don't remember anything else. "What is it?" I finally ask.

"My head of security will take you to the jail."

Fuck.

"The Escalade is waiting for you outside."

Nick ends the call, and I think I'm going to be sick.

If Andre drives, I won't be able to make the exchange with Edna. And it's not like I can bring both Bibles with me. I can't bring a gun inside the prison.

After I see Carmelo, Andre will take me to the meet with Nick. Once Nick gets what he wants, without the gun, I will have no way to protect my brother, no way to protect myself. Tommy and I will be loose ends.

And mobsters don't like loose ends.

Vomit burns the back of my throat. I give in to it and puke into the sink.

When I'm empty, Edna hands me a paper towel.

I wipe my mouth, hands shaking.

"Bet you wish you listened to me now," Edna says.

I think about Edna's warning about Tommy, what she said after church yesterday. And it feels like a lifetime ago. "Now you decide to rub it in."

She shrugs. "It's not my style, but when you're right, you're right."

I laugh, but my hands continue to shake.

She finds her purse, pulls out a flask, pushes it to me. "This will take the edge off."

"I can't go to the jail smelling like booze."

"Please. The way that place smells. No one will notice."

I take a drink. The whiskey burns my throat.

I think about Andre waiting outside. I don't want him to look for me. I don't want him to see Edna here. I need to move. I cap the flask and hand it back to her.

"I'll figure out a way to get you the gun, Viv."

There won't be a window, not with Andre babysitting me. "It's too late, Edna."

"It's only too late, when you're pushing up dirt."

I reach down and pet Reggie. Then, I hug Edna like I'm never going to see her again.

"Look for my signal, Viv."

I love her tenacity. I just can't see how she's going to pull it off. But I nod anyway.

Then, I take the Bible—the one without the gun—and I head outside to face The Giant.

Andre is at the curb with the Escalade like Nick promised. He's leaning against the driver's side, arms folded. He seems taller, bigger.

If that's even possible.

He pats me down, the same routine as before. He fans through the Bible and confiscates my cell phone.

It takes forty minutes to reach the prison. Getting through security is easy and accessing Carmelo is easy, too.

Don't get me wrong, there are things about jail that aren't easy for me. The sound of the security buzzer, the clang of the doors, the smell of metal and sweat—basically anything that triggers memories from my first stint.

But these things don't bother me.

Not today.

I'm more anxious about Nick and what he'll do to Tommy than demons of my own.

When I reach Carmelo's cell. I can see him through a small plexiglass window. He's different than I expect. Not big or muscular like Andre. He's slight, withered. Maybe it's from old age or the time he's spent in the can. But he looks more like a bean counter and less like a hitman. He actually wants to talk. He tells me about The Life, the things that brought him here.

His regret.

I listen, talk about God. Then, I do what Nick asks and pass him the Bible with the Saint Anthony pamphlet inside. He flips through it, reads some scripture aloud. Psalm 23:4. And I wonder if he's worried about dying.

God knows I am.

Then, he returns everything to me.

At least that's how it appears.

An hour later, I exit the turnstile of the prison gate. The sun outside is too bright, too hot.

Sweat pulls under my armpits. I wonder what's going to happen next.

Will Andre deliver me to Nick?

Will I see Tommy?

Will Nick kill us both?

I scan the parking lot. Look for Edna's car. Hope that she's here. That she's pulled off some kind of miracle.

But there's no powder-blue Oldsmobile.

There's is no Edna.

There's just Andre waiting with the Escalade.

He climbs out and opens the rear passenger door.

I suck in a breath and start toward the SUV, gravel crunching under my feet like some kind of death knell.

I'm nearly at the Escalade when I see it.

Edna's signal.

It's Reggie.

And he's running straight at me.

I blink. Look for Edna. Find her trailing behind Reggie—a version
of her anyway. She's wearing a hat and the hoodie from the Lost
and Found along with her prescription sunglasses and her
purse. It's slung in the crook of her arm.

"I'm sorry," she yells, her voice frantic. "Damn dog. I'm sor—"

But I don't hear the rest. Reggie jumps and crashes into me.
The Bible tumbles out of my hand. I stumble back and slam
against the ground. The Pitbull is on top of me now. He licks
my face. I raise my hands and pretend to fight him off.

"Are you okay?" Edna asks panting from running. She drops
to the ground, her body between me and the Escalade. "My
Beaufort is getting released today, and I promised I'd bring the
dog. I knew it was a mistake. The uncivilized beast."

Edna continues to drone on. I'm not sure what she does
next, if she's able to make the switch, because my focus is on
Andre. I see him over Edna's shoulder, lumbering toward us.

He reaches for Reggie's collar and pulls the Pitbull off of me.

"Thank you," Edna says while she watches Andre struggle
with the dog. "If you don't mind." She hands Andre the dog's
leash.

While Andre fights to hook up Reggie, Edna helps me to my
feet. Then, she picks up the Bible with a Saint Anthony pamphlet
tucked inside. Makes a show of brushing it off before she hands
it to me. The book feels different, weighty.

And I know the Tokarev is there.

I pull the Bible tighter to my chest and thank God Tommy
and I have a fighting chance.

I glance around for the Bible with Carmelo's information,
but it's already tucked inside Edna's purse.

More brushing from Edna—she's working on my clothes.
When she's done, she looks at me, the way she does when she

wants to make sure I'm listening.

"I hope you'll forgive me," she says.

The remorse in her voice sounds heartfelt, and even I'm impressed with her Oscar-winning performance.

Andre finally manages to connect Reggie's leash, and he hands the Pitbull over to Edna.

I linger, not wanting to leave, not wanting to face Nick. "Good luck with Beaufort."

"We need to go." Andre pushes me toward the Escalade.

As we drive away, I look at Edna, purse in the crook of her arm, Reggie obediently by her side—not knowing she betrayed me.

Andre and I meet Nick at the port on Lake Michigan.

And I know this can't be good.

I see Tommy. He's on his knees, hands tied behind his back, flanked by a pair of Nick's goons.

I get out of the Escalade, Bible clutched to my chest. When Andre and I approach Nick, Tommy lifts his head and looks at me.

He's scared. I can see it in his eyes. It's the same look he gave me the day social services took us from our mother. I flash a reassuring smile even though I'm scared, too. Just like I did when we were kids.

"How did it go?" Nick asks.

"Carmelo sends his regards," I tell him, not sure what to say.

Nick snaps his fingers, motions for Andre to bring him the trifold.

The Giant lumbers toward me.

Five steps away...

There are so many things riding on what happens next.

Will Nick be willing to negotiate—Tommy's life for Carmelo's information? Or will he simply kill us both?

Three steps...

I pray Tommy knows how much I love him. That he gave my life purpose. How he was the reason I was able to survive my darkest hours.

Two...

I tell my brother I love him.

One...

I reach for the gun.

"You're talking about the Tokarev?" the Fed with the buzz cut asks.

I nod.

"I need you to respond for the recording."

"Yes."

His eyes narrow.

"I pulled the Tokarev."

He flips through his notes. "The gun you purchased from the taco truck."

"We've been through this already." To think I actually slipped this clown some cash—that he played me with his homeless act. It still pisses me off.

"I want to go through it again."

I lean forward in my chair, slide my hands across the table, the silver bracelets on my wrists digging into my skin, and reach for the bottle of water. I manage to unscrew the cap, hold the bottle, take a sip. "I pulled the Tokarev," I tell Buzz Cut. "The same gun I purchased from the taco truck."

"The gun the woman known as Eastside Edna helped you buy?"

Just hearing her name makes me sick.

"I need you to respond for the—"

"Edna told me about the truck."

"After you pulled the gun, what happened next?"

"You tell me, you were there."

My mind goes back to Buzz Cut and his team of Feds. How

they rolled up in their sedans in a brown blaze of glory and arrested me and Tommy, along with Nick and the rest of his crew.

How Edna tipped them off.

I wonder when they squeezed her, how long she'd been giving them information. Were we ever truly friends? Or was I simply a way for her to protect her bookie business?

Was I her self-preservation card?

I like to think we were friends. I like to think the warnings about Tommy, the times she told me to walk away that she was trying to protect me. But who knows. It could have been her way of gaining my trust. What I do know is that the street kid in me was right.

Kindness is always a prelude to pain.

Buzz Cut's stomach rumbles. He glances at his watch. "It's getting late. Let's pick this up tomorrow." He turns off the video camera and signals someone through the one-way mirror to come get me.

"Remember our deal," I remind him. "My testimony in exchange for WITSEC."

"I showed you the signed agreement. The Marshals have already moved Tommy and Arlene to a safe house. Between your testimony and the information from Carmelo, it should be enough to keep Nick and his crew locked up for a long time."

It turns out Carmelo wasn't a geriatric hitman but an accountant for the mob. He stashed mob assets across the country—guns, jewelry, and cash—all evidence tied to multiple crimes.

Nick knew the Feds were closing in. He used me to get the stash house locations from Carmelo hoping he could beat the Feds there.

"So, Tommy's safe?" I need to hear Buzz Cut say it again.

Buzz Cut nods. "He's safe."

"That's all I ever wanted."

* * *

I'm in my cell when they come for me. I hear them before I see them—the hushed voices, the unfamiliar footsteps. And I can't say I'm surprised.

Rule #3—and all that.

The guard unlocks the door and walks away.

I think about Tommy, the life I've always wanted for him, for his kid. I imagine him safe in a house in the burbs with a steady job and a family who sits around the table for Sunday dinners. I imagine I have a seat at the table, too.

I pray this time he works on that new leaf and turns his life around. I take a deep breath and close my eyes, right before the blade is pressed against my throat.

GUNS+TACOS CREATED AND EDITED BY | MICHAEL BRACKEN & TREY R. BARKER

DAVID H. HENDRICKSON

CHIMICHANGAS
AND A COUPLE OF GLOCKS

SEASON **3** GUNS+TACOS EPISODE **15**

OTHER TITLES BY DAVID H. HENDRICKSON

Cracking the Ice
Offside
Offensive Foul
Bottom of the Ninth
Bubba Goes for Broke
Body Check
No Defense

Omnibus Editions
The Rabbit Labelle Trilogy

Short Story Collections
Shimmers and Laughs: Eight Wildly Hilarious Tales
Death in the Serengeti and Other Stories: Ten Tales of Crime
The Boy in the Boxers and Other Stories of Sweet Romance
Hell of a Band: Twelve Fantasy Stories

Nonfiction
How to Get Your Book into Schools and Double Your Income
with Volume Sales
Travis Roy: Quadriplegia and a Life of Purpose

CHIMICHANGAS AND A COUPLE OF GLOCKS

David H. Hendrickson

To Michael Bracken
For the opportunity

Peter looked terrified and he *never* looked like that. That scared the living daylights out of Lizzie Hosker. In the eight months she'd known him, and the four months they'd lived together, she'd never seen him even the least bit frightened. He was always cocky as hell with his thick, dark hair, his muscular build, and blue eyes. His snug designer jeans and dress shirts fit him just right, the top three buttons on his shirts left unbuttoned to show a thin, gold chain nestled in his black chest hair.

Cocky, always. And why wouldn't he be? Frightened, never.

Lizzie knew what other people thought when they saw the two of them together: *what the hell does he see in her?* He had the movie star good looks and the bright smile; she was Plain Jane. Scrawny, barely five feet tall, flat-chested, and mousy. Drab, brown hair that just hung there, not quite to her shoulders. Boring brown eyes. As glamorous as cardboard. Yet they were engaged to be married. The ultimate odd couple.

She sat at the circular kitchen table, facing the apartment's front door, her textbooks fanned out in a semi-circle atop the plain white tablecloth, her laptop centered in the middle. A junior year pre-med at the University of Chicago, she was studying for her Pathogenic Bacteriology and Immunology exam next week. It was the first week of October, a month into what UC referred to as the Autumn Quarter, and she already knew the textbook inside and out, had her notes memorized, and was at least a week ahead in all of her other studies. But you could never be too prepared.

The smell of garlic bread and lasagna—Peter's favorite— filled the kitchen, emanating from the oven behind her. To her left, the refrigerator hummed beside a sink and stove. Though she'd been a vegetarian for years prior to meeting Peter, she made the lasagna with sweet Italian sausage because that was how he liked it.

And what Peter liked, Peter got. She couldn't even pick out the pieces of sausage of her own slice of lasagna. The one time she'd tried that had infuriated Peter, and he'd made her pay. It had been painful to sit for a week.

Never again.

So tonight she would follow all his rules to the letter, eat the pieces of meat, smile at the right time, laugh at his jokes, and maybe for a change they could actually *make love*, not that other stuff. Actually kiss and share nice romantic gestures like in the movies, like she'd heard people engaged to be married did.

Not that other stuff.

A girl could dream, couldn't she?

But all such dreams flew out the window when Peter burst through the front door and slammed it behind him. Lizzie looked up and tried her prettiest smile, knowing full well it really wasn't pretty at all. But it was the best she had.

Her painfully ordinary smile faltered, then was gone.

Peter was in trouble. *Big* trouble. Had to be. His eyes were wild, his breathing ragged. Beads of sweat formed on his forehead as he stood across the table from her.

"What's wrong?" Lizzie cried, trying to get to her feet but falling back into her chair, her legs suddenly weak.

"You've got to help me," Peter said, and took a big gulp of air. "I've got a…got an *emergency*. You gotta help."

Was it money again? Peter always needed money. He was *always* broke, and it was always an emergency. She paid for everything. The apartment. The food. The last four payments on his Acura. He would say he needed the money, she would pay, and that was that. It was, she thought, an investment in their future together.

But the requests for money—that somewhere in the back of her mind she acknowledged were actually demands—had never come like this. Not with panicked eyes. Or rasping breath. Or such obvious fear. At least no fear on *his* part. He would smile and ask nicely, cajoling her, laying on the charm, pointing out that eventually when that diamond ring she wore—a ring she'd also paid for, though she would deny that humiliating fact to her dying day—when it was joined by a wedding ring, their money would all be shared anyway. So what difference did it make?

He'd be sweet, or at least as sweet as Peter ever got. Not frightened like this.

"What trouble are you in?" Lizzie asked.

Peter shook his head. "Better you didn't know."

"Peter, you're scaring me," Lizzie said, her heart pounding even harder than when Peter made his other demands.

He stepped to the table, reached across it, and grabbed her by the shoulders. Tight. So tight it hurt.

"You need to do this," he said, shaking her. "Now put on your big girl pants and listen to me."

Lizzie nodded. Tears pooled in her eyes, but she held them back, blinking rapidly. Peter hated when she cried at times like these. Crying was only for their *playtime*, as he called it.

"There's a truck where you're going to pick up something

for me," Peter said, his eyes trying to lock onto hers even as she looked away. "*Look at me!*" he roared, and pulled back a strong, hard hand to hit her.

"No!" she yelped. "I mean, yes!"

Lizzie looked into Peter's dark, cold eyes. She thought they were like a serpent's eyes. Her chest thundered. She tried to breathe, but couldn't.

"Okay, now," Peter said, lowering his hand. He exhaled noisily through his nose, then ran his fingers through his hair. "You're going to pick up a package for me."

Lizzie wanted to cry. "*Drugs?*"

"No, not drugs, you stupid bitch!" Peter said with a shake of his head.

Lizzie hated when he called her a bitch, but at least it wasn't the C word. And of course, calling her a stupid bitch didn't make any sense, not when she had a 4.0 GPA in pre-med, and he was barely staying afloat in Business Management. He didn't apply himself. Skipped too many classes. But she knew she couldn't say a word of that in reply. She'd better not let even the hint of the thought cross her face.

So she just looked at him, trying desperately to keep her face blank.

"It's something to protect me," Peter said.

"Protect you?"

"*Is there a fucking echo in here?*"

Lizzie shook her head furiously. She couldn't imagine what trouble Peter was in or what she might get to protect him, but she'd learned long ago, long before she even met Peter, to do what she was told and keep her mouth shut.

"Okay," Peter said. "It's going to cost several hundred dollars. Maybe even close to a thousand. So bring a thousand just in case. Cash."

"A thousand dollars?" Lizzie asked, the words slipping out before she could stop them. "Peter what is happening? What do you need a thousand dollars for to protect you?"

Anger filled Peter's eyes. Lizzie cringed. She was sure she was going to pay for not keeping her mouth shut. But this time she got lucky. He just shook his head and replied through clenched teeth.

"This is to keep me alive. Do you think I'm worth it, or is that too much for you?"

"Of course! I'm sorry." Lizzie swallowed hard. "What do I need to do?"

"You're going to go find this truck and a guy named Jesse. Sometime after ten tonight. Between ten and four in the morning."

"Four in the morning?" Lizzie felt her eyes widen, despite her best attempts not to show any reaction. She had an eight a.m. class, though she certainly couldn't say that. Couldn't even think it and was ashamed of herself for doing so. This was her fiancée! Her future husband! How could she even think about her classes and being tired and preserving her perfect 4.0 GPA? This was to keep Peter alive. She was such a horrible, horrible person. She deserved every last punishment he meted out on her.

"And it's...it's not going to be in a good part of town," Peter said, fortunately not reading her thoughts.

"Where?" Lizzie asked, holding her breath.

"Somewhere near Fuller Park."

Ooof! The words came as a slap, every bit as hard as the ones he applied to her bottom during *playtime*. Lizzie almost wet her pants. Fuller Park was the most dangerous part of Chicago. The murder capital of the city. She'd never once dared to step foot even close to it.

"*Fuller Park?*" she said feebly, knowing she should keep her big mouth shut but unable to help herself.

"Yeah, you're going to do it, and you aren't going to be a baby about it!"

Lizzie nodded, trying to look brave, trying to feel brave, but failing on all counts. Her mind raced. *Fuller Park, Fuller Park, Fuller Park!* And then, *between ten at night and four in the morning! In Fuller Park!* She couldn't breathe. Couldn't swallow.

Finally, she managed, "What kind of truck?"

"A taco truck," Peter said.

Lizzie stared at him for a moment, not comprehending, and then it hit her. *A taco truck!* Relief washed over her. All the tension and fear that had been tightening and tightening like a clenched fist burst free. *Taco truck!* She had all she could do to keep from bursting out in laughter. Only the memory of what had happened the last time Peter thought she was laughing at him stopped her.

But it was hard to hold back the belly laugh. All this talk of taking a thousand dollars into Fuller Park—*a thousand dollars into Fuller Park in the dead of night!*—and Peter's Oscar-worthy performance of fearing for his life, it had all been nothing more than an elaborate ruse to again bring up her big mistake. To again pressure her for a threesome.

"Is that all this is?" she asked. "You're just teasing me about tacos again?"

The word "taco" had caused so much pain between the two of them. Well, had caused so much pain for *her.* Peter called it teasing, and she tried to convince herself that that's all it was, but it was tormenting, no doubt about it. He knew it and she knew it.

He'd had to explain it to her at first. A "sausage fest" was a party where there were almost all guys; a "taco fest" was one were there were almost all women. Even then, she still hadn't gotten it. Her, a 4.0 pre-med student. He'd had to connect the dots. Penis to sausage; vulva—or as he put it, "pussy"—to taco.

She'd felt her face redden at the explanation back then and even more when he continually rubbed her nose in it, reminding her—ridiculing her—for that *one time*, for that *one mistake*. For the one time she'd "gone taco." Been with a woman.

Even though it really had been his fault.

The night that ended their relationship, though not forever, Lizzie thought they were having sex in their normal way. Which was anything but normal, but was normal for her and Peter. Giving him what he wanted, what he needed. And maybe she needed it, too, although she felt so perpetually conflicted and guilty about sex that she really wasn't sure what she wanted or what she needed.

It had been that way since she was eleven when Uncle Bob did those things to her. Touching her in her private, dirty places. Then blaming her and threatening to tell her parents if she said a word to anyone.

And when she did remain silent, he did even more things.

For three years.

Until her mother caught the two of them.

And though her mother did threaten to cut Uncle Bob's penis off with a steak knife, she saved the lion's share of the blame for Lizzie. *How could you let a man do that to you? Why did you tempt Uncle Bob, who is a church-going, God-fearing man, with a wife and three kids of his own! What kind of a shameful* slut *are you to have done all of that? What is* wrong *with you?*

Lizzie had been trying to figure out what was wrong with her ever since.

In quiet. That was the ironclad rule, back then and to this day. No one else was to know. Not her father. Not Uncle Bob's wife. There was no need to ruin his marriage. No need to cast shame on her three cousins when she, Lizzie, was the one to blame. No one was to know! And certainly no therapist, a stranger for God's sake!

She was to keep her mouth shut, her legs closed, and stop looking and acting like a whore. Maybe then, if she was lucky, no one else but the three of them would ever find out about the terrible things she had done. No one else would have to know what a horrible little girl she was. What a tramp. An embarrassment to herself and to her family and to all of God's creation.

Perhaps, if she told no one, she could even forget it herself. Pretend it had never happened. Make sure nothing like it ever happened again. She wouldn't even *dare* to look pretty and seduce an innocent man. Look as ugly as she could, stay away from all boys, and certainly all men, so she would never tempt them again. And maybe if it never happened again, her horrible secret would be buried like a decaying corpse and no one would ever have to know that it was even there. That it had ever been there.

Not even she would remember.

So Lizzie kept her mouth shut and tried to bury it. But her shameful secret crawled out of the moist earth like a decaying corpse from the horror movies to remind her what a horrible person—what a sinful, shameful, depraved little girl who didn't deserve to live—she was.

Over and over. The decaying corpse of her secret crawled out and pointed a skeletal finger at her. She was just a shameful slut. A tramp who had tricked a married man, her uncle, into having sex with her.

She was a horrible, horrible person, no matter how many straight-A report cards she got. No matter that she made herself as unattractive as possible. No matter that she made absolutely sure she didn't accidentally seduce any married men. No matter that she didn't date any boys, ever.

She was a horrible person and always would be. That skeletal finger would forever point at her and remind her of her shame.

Until Peter.

Peter saw something in her that first day at the library. And he told her she was pretty! Lizzie was sure he was mocking her. Of course, he was mocking her. Boys had been doing that for years.

And even if Peter wasn't, Lizzie didn't want to be pretty. She wasn't supposed to be pretty. Pretty was what had ruined her life.

But Peter persisted. He wasn't mocking her. He told her she really was pretty! And he could release that inner beauty of hers if only she would let him.

The beauty of pain, he told her on their third date. Punishing what was bad inside her—and *so much* was bad inside her!—so she could be free.

He could make her happy. Through *playtime*. Sometimes he called it *pain-time*. He could grant her freedom through pain.

Perhaps, Lizzie told herself, every punishment was beating that decaying corpse and its accusatory skeletal finger. Beating the corpse into submission even as she submitted to Peter's hand.

The theory was working, at least as well as any theory had worked for Lizzie, until the night two months ago, two months after Peter had moved in with her, when it almost ended forever.

It had begun with the usual spanking. Sometimes, Peter preferred that she wear her tightest pair of jeans and the spanking would start that way. More often, though, he preferred a dress, and that was the case that night. He sat on their queen-sized, four-poster bed, the walnut headboard to his left, the matching dressers to his right. Nightstands with lamps turned down low, but not off, bracketed the two sides of the bed. The woody, musky scent of sex candles filled the air.

Peter pulled up her dress, bent her over his lap, and began to spank, first with her underwear still on, then with it pulled down. As his palm slapped harder and harder, and the stinging of her bottom hurt more and more, Peter told her what an awful, shameful slut she was—reminding her what she already knew, what she could never forget—but by taking her punishment, she was becoming beautiful.

Then he took off all her clothes, applied a black, satin blindfold and a cloth gag, and threw her onto the bed, calling her "his dirty slut," which was surely true. He tied her wrists and ankles tightly to the four posts with the well-worn, clothesline-thick rope he always used. She yelped with the pain she knew she deserved with every pinch of her nipples and every slap of her inner thighs. She groaned in the way she knew Peter liked when he played with her down there.

Then came the hot wax from the candles. Not ordinary candles, of course, which would leave second-degree burns and could send someone to the hospital. Peter wasn't an animal. He also wasn't a novice. He knew what he was doing. And as each drop splattered onto her skin, hurting terribly but the pain so very much deserved and really not that much more intense than the rest of their repertoire, Peter repeated his mantra.

"Take it, you dirty bitch! Take it!"

Nothing at all out of the ordinary. Just what Lizzie had come to expect. Giving Peter what he needed. Taking whatever he decided to give her, whatever he decided she needed.

After a short break, during which the hot wax hardened and she grew more and more nervous, wondering what would happen next, Peter began taking photographs with what sounded like his iPhone. Lizzie didn't like that. If he ever got tired of her—a frightening possibility she had to at least consider even though they were engaged—he might not want to give the photographs back. He'd taken photos before, but when she protested nicely afterwards, had promised he'd deleted them.

But here he was taking photographs again. A *lot* of them.

Click! Click! Click! Click!

Lizzie shook her head in protest—something she never did—but Peter seemed to take the photos even faster.

Click! Click! Click! Click! Click! Click! Click! Click!

Impossibly fast.

Click! Click! Click! Click! Click! Click! Click! Click! Click! Click! Click! Click!

She shook her head more forcefully.

"Do what I say!" he commanded.

And then he took off the blindfold.

There, hovering over her, taking pictures with their phones, were three other men at the foot of the bed. Strangers she had never seen before.

Pants and underwear either down at their ankles, or off entirely, Lizzie couldn't see.

Fully erect.

Lizzie screamed through her wet cloth gag.

"She's all yours, boys," Peter said with a smile and a gleam in his eyes.

"No!" Lizzie screamed through the gag. She shook her head fiercely from side to side. *"NO!"*

One of them hesitated. He had short blond hair and tattoos all across his chest and upper arms.

"You said she wanted this!" he said to Peter.

"She does!" Peter said, eyes wild.

He turned to Lizzie, grabbed her chin tightly, and said, "Tell them you really want it!"

But *no, no, no,* she couldn't do that. She may be a horrible person and a shameful slut—she was!—but she couldn't do that!

Lizzie shook her head *no, no, no.* As best she could through the cloth gag, she tried to scream, *"Rape!"*

As the other two strangers stood there, saying nothing, looking at each other, the blond grabbed Peter and shoved him.

"What the fuck are you trying to do? Set us up to go to jail for life?"

"No, she wants it!" Peter said.

The blond man narrowed his eyes. "Let's see."

When he loosened the knot on the back of the gag and it fell free, Lizzie let loose a blood-curdling scream that left no doubt.

"You fucking asshole!" the naked blond man said, getting his face right in Peter's. "You fucking asshole!"

"She said this was what she wanted," Peter said, spreading his hands wide, a look of innocence on his face even as Lizzie demanded to be set free. Peter clamped a hand down on her mouth. "She's been talking about it for weeks. This was her secret fantasy she wanted to come true. Swear to God! She must have changed her mind."

Lizzie stayed the next three nights in a tiny studio apartment with an old classmate named Julie O'Meara. Average height and shape, Julie had curly, light-brown hair, brown eyes, and had always been friendly with a warm smile back when they took classes together freshman year. They'd never been close friends—Lizzie didn't do that close friends sort of thing—and they'd barely seen each other after Julie dropped out of pre-med and shifted to something less demanding. But Julie's was the first familiar face Lizzie bumped into after fleeing her apartment barefoot, hair askew, tears streaming down her face, and blouse misbuttoned.

Lizzie told Julie nothing of what had just happened—old habits die hard, even the worst of them—only that she needed a place to stay for a couple nights. Lizzie offered to sleep on the floor—there was only the tiny bedroom, bathroom, and kitchen—but Julie insisted that they could squeeze into her twin bed, and they did. Lizzie did her best not to disrupt her host's sleep, fighting off the urge to break into a crying jag and trembling fits that might never end.

On the second night, Lizzie lay in bed beneath the covers, eyes closed, her back flat against the wall so she'd take up as little space on the tiny bed as possible, and counted silently down from a hundred to try to calm her breathing and hold off the urge to cry.

She felt soft lips upon hers. Gently kissing her.

Lizzie's eyes shot open wide. Her whole body became rigid. "*What are you doing?*"

"Shhh!" Julie said, and held a finger to Lizzie's lips.

"I'm not—"

"Something's wrong, I can tell. Let me make you feel better," Julie said.

Lizzie didn't move. This wasn't her. She wasn't a lesbian. She was sure of it. She was all kinds of awful things. Her mother had been right about them all. And being a lesbian wouldn't be awful at all. Especially after what had just happened. She never wanted to see a man again.

But she wasn't a lesbian.

Still, Lizzie didn't want to seem rude to her host. And maybe she could learn to be a lesbian.

And never have a man in her life again. Never a man like Peter. The thought of him made her shudder, which Julie took as encouragement. Never men like those three strangers who, all but her blond rescuer, were going to follow Peter's biding and prove once and for all—if it ever needed proof—what a shameful, worthless, filthy slut Lizzie really was.

She shuddered again.

Julie moved lower until her kisses were *down there*. Tender kisses. Something totally unfamiliar to Lizzie.

Oooh-boy. Lizzie didn't know what to think. Except that she didn't deserve this.

It was too...too loving. *Loving?* Sensual without being painful.

No, she certainly didn't deserve this. She was a totally worthless piece of dung. Deserving of nothing but getting her bottom whipped. Her mother had been right about everything. Heck, Lizzie had almost seduced three strangers into gang-raping her. What more proof was needed?

But Julie was...*oooh-boy.*

Oooh-boy.

Oooh-boy.

After a lot of *oooh-boys*, Lizzie guiltily tried to reciprocate. Though Julie told her to take this slow, that would be for another night, Lizzie knew she didn't deserve to be on the receiving end of pleasure. That only proved her mother had been right. And Lizzie certainly couldn't take and not give back. That was being the most wanton slut of all.

She was supposed to give pleasure, not take it. Like she'd given so much to Peter so many times. Not receiving pleasure except in pain.

So she tried to give pleasure to Julie, and though Julie responded with encouraging moans, it still felt all wrong to Lizzie. She just wasn't wired that way. She could force herself to do it, like she forced herself to do things for Peter. But this just wasn't her.

119

Lizzie heard her mother's accusing voice. First, Uncle Bob, a God-fearing, married man with three kids. Then three men ready to ravish her all at the same time. Now with a woman. *Enjoying it with a woman.* Sodom and Gomorrah had nothing over the wanton whore that Lizzie had become.

Peter found out about the episode on their sixth day back together. And never let her forget it.

Lizzie hadn't intended to reconcile with him. She'd blocked his repeated calls, first on his regular phone and then what must be a burner. She wanted no part of him ever again. The horror of those three strangers standing beside the bed, prepared to…prepared to…

Ooof!

Lizzie shuddered as she walked down the suddenly long, fourth-floor halfway to her apartment door on the left. *Yea though I walk through the valley of the shadow of death* flashed through her mind. She didn't want to be here. Didn't want to think about what had happened in that apartment bedroom. Didn't want to recall Peter's words urging the strangers on.

She never wanted to see Peter again.

But she had to get her things. She could replace her clothes. Might actually want to burn anything Peter had touched. But she needed her heavily highlighted textbooks and her laptop, which held all her detailed notes. There was only so much she'd been able to do at the library and on its computers. It was amazing she'd lasted almost three days without her books and laptop.

If only she'd been able to grab them as she fled the scene that night. Then she'd never need to return to the apartment again. Get the lease cancelled and never step foot in *the valley of the shadow of death.* But she'd had all she could do to throw on her clothes and run like hell barefoot from Peter and those men.

There was nothing fortunate about that night with the three

strangers. Nothing. Except of course that the blond one had refused to...refused to...

Ooof!

Lizzie shuddered again. She tried to push that image if not away—those things never, ever truly left—but push it into that buried deep part of her mind with Uncle Bob and...

Ooof! Go away!

Lizzie tried to clear her thoughts. At least that awful night—*ooof! ooof! ooof!*—at least it had happened on a Friday so she'd had no classes the next two days. But now it was Monday morning and she had no choice but to retrieve her books and laptop.

With any luck, Peter wouldn't be here. Or at least he'd be sleeping so soundly he wouldn't hear her—it was barely after six in the morning—and she could grab her things. He'd never know she'd been there. As long as she had her books and laptop, she could find somewhere else to stay. Maybe she could even go back to Julie and learn to be a lesbian. Lizzie doubted it, but maybe she hadn't given it enough time.

No, she'd just find another apartment. She did have *some* money left. Her parents had both passed away in recent years, and as an only child, she'd inherited what little there was to inherit. But Peter had been plowing through that money at an alarming rate. It wouldn't last forever. And unfortunately, the apartment was in her name, and it had been her security deposit. If Peter trashed the place, she'd be responsible for it.

She had to kick Peter out, didn't she? And how could she ever do that? She'd never ordered him to do anything. And if he refused, which of course he would, then what could she do? She wasn't about to call the police and have to explain what had happened.

What a mess she'd made. And of course, she deserved it all. Awful things happened to awful people.

Holding her breath, Lizzie turned the key in the lock. The clicking sound roared in her ears. It echoed down the cavernous, empty hallway. She tiptoed inside.

She let her eyes adjust to the dim light, the darkness broken only by the early morning sunlight streaming in the six-foot-wide living room window on the right.

Peter was in the apartment—of course he was!—sleeping in the bedroom off to the back left, its door wide open. Lizzie listened to his slight snore. Perhaps she might get lucky after all and pull off a clean getaway. In and out of the apartment in less than five minutes, with Peter never knowing she'd even been here.

But since when did Lizzie Hosker ever get lucky? When did it ever make sense for her to hope for anything? Her books and laptop were nowhere to be found.

Of course.

They'd been on the circular kitchen table when she'd fled—*for her life!*—on Friday night. Now, she tiptoed through the kitchen, checking the cabinets, atop the refrigerator, even somewhat absurdly, in the oven. Then through the living room, beneath and behind the couch, on the coffee table, and then...

Into the windowless bedroom. Darker than the rest of the apartment.

Where Peter still slept, smelling of alcohol, though no longer snoring, on the four-poster bed. Where the three strangers had stood around her as she lay there helpless...

Ooof!

Lizzie's heart jackhammered. She fought back a jagged cry. Held her breath. And got down on all fours to look under the bed. At first, it was too dark to see, but then in the shadows more than an arm's length away...

Jackpot!

Three stacks of books and, to their left, the laptop.

Holding her breath, Lizzie flattened herself against the carpet. She reached far beneath the bed, just barely touching the first stack. As silently as she possible, she slowly slid it toward her.

Got it.

Two more to go plus the laptop. Her nose began to twitch

with the dust she'd raised, so she opted to get the laptop next. Just in case she had to make a run for it. The laptop with all her notes and completed assignments was the top priority. If she'd been thinking, she would have gotten it first, but who could think at times like this? She got it out, though, and was reaching for the next stack when a strong, warm hand touched the back of her neck.

Lizzie screamed.

The hand's grasp tightened for an instant, then released its grip.

"Why don't you answer my calls?" Peter asked.

Lizzie lay there unmoving. Unable to speak.

"You treat me like I'm a monster," he said.

And you are! Lizzie thought, but certainly couldn't say it. She swallowed hard and just lay there. Helpless again. Such a familiar feeling.

"I was only doing what I thought you wanted," Peter said, calmly and reasonably. Like a stockbroker describing investments. "Everything we've always done has been to give you what you want. Give you what you need."

What I want? What I need? How could you ever think that's what I wanted?

But again, she couldn't speak the thoughts aloud. Only lay there, his firm hand still upon the back of her neck, holding her down but only loosely. The rough fabric of the carpet scratched her nose. Its slight musty scent filled her nostrils.

"I only wanted to please you," Peter said. "It was the logical next step."

Please me?

"I love you, Lizzie."

The makeup sex almost made her late for her nine o'clock class. She'd been such a fool to think that Peter would have forced the three men on her if he hadn't truly thought that had been what she secretly wanted.

In fact, he had to punish her for even thinking that of him. And for thinking he would allow those three men to leave the apartment without deleting their photos of her. What kind of monster did she think he was? So many evil thoughts of her to punish! So many punishments that she deserved.

The makeup sex resumed that night after dinner at Ruth's Chris Steak House on North Dearborn. Lizzie paid with her credit card, of course, since Peter had no money. And most vegetarians, even lapsed ones, preferred other restaurants than steak houses.

But it was the thought that counted. And the thoughts of hers that required atonement. She definitely deserved the extra-hard spankings that night and the tight nipple clamps.

But Peter really sealed the deal the next night when he got down on one knee and proposed, albeit with a ring from a bubble gum machine.

"We are so right for each other," he said. "I want to spend the rest of my life with you and only you. Will you marry me?"

Shocked—*stunned!*—Lizzie said yes. Of course, she said yes!

Two nights later, they went shopping for a real ring, a half-carat diamond. Lizzie felt euphoric, even as she signed the credit card slip.

That night, Peter tied her up face down and gave Lizzie what she truly deserved. But with extra lube, of course.

On the weekend, while bent over Peter's lap getting spanked, she let slip about her experience with Julie.

"Were you with any other men while we were apart?" Peter asked, his breathing heavy.

Lizzie, who could never be a poker player because she was the worst liar in the world, said no, but something in her voice betrayed her.

"*Lizzie?*" he asked and brought his hand down hard.

Peter got the truth out of her minutes later.

"You taco-loving slut!" he said gleefully.

* * *

Peter had been tormenting her as a "taco lover" ever since—"Lizzie the Lesbo!"—along with demands that she set up a "taco party" for him, a threesome with her and Julie. Or a suitable substitute.

Lizzie always gave in to Peter's demands. Always. But their agreement even before their engagement, their agreement even as she lay face down on the bedroom floor with Peter's hand on her neck and the carpet fabric scraping her nose, was that there would be no one else. He could have his way with her and give her what punishments he wanted—"what you need!" he had said—but never again would there be anyone else in the bedroom with them.

Even she had her limits. No three strangers. No Julie, or anyone else.

She was not Lizzie the Lesbo, no matter what Peter said. Though that didn't stop him from bringing up her "love for tacos" and the possibility of a "taco party" for him on an almost daily basis.

So two months later, relief washed over her after Peter scared the living daylights out of her with his talk of him being in grave danger only to have it be nothing more than an elaborate gag to once again torment her about her mistake.

Taco truck!

Peter being Peter. Lizzie just wondered about the exact term. If a taco party was multiple women, then what was a taco truck? Big women?

But, no, it turned out that a taco truck really meant...a taco truck.

Lizzie gripped the ten-year-old Hyundai's steering wheel so tightly her knuckles turned white. Her heart jackhammered, threating to explode out of her chest. She tried to swallow but couldn't. Felt a bitter taste in her mouth and down her throat.

Ooof! Fuller Park! And in the pitch-black darkness of midnight, no less. With fifteen hundred dollars in her pocket—Peter had told her a thousand, but she'd brought extra, just in case—practically asking to be robbed and even worse. Why weren't there more working streetlights? Fuller Park had a scary reputation even in broad daylight. Darkness made it even more menacing. She'd never once stepped foot in the neighborhood and had intended to always keep it that way.

It wasn't Fuller Park's racial makeup. It was all the murders. And here she was—she, who hardly ever ventured outside of her apartment and the UC campus—driving through it in the dead of midnight.

Dead was what she'd be lucky not to be an hour from now. Or maybe she might even be wishing she were dead. *Ooof!* She checked that the car doors were locked for perhaps the tenth time as she drove by seven or eight young men sitting on the stoop of yet another boarded-up house.

Lizzie held her breath and kept driving, looking straight ahead even while checking with her peripheral vision to make sure that no one was running at the car from the side. Ready to smash in the windows and drag her from the car.

Ooof!

House after house was boarded up, their small yards overrun with knee-high weeds. Graffiti covered the walls of abandoned warehouses. More streetlights were burned out or broken, giving the orange glow cast by those that worked an even more haunting look.

The fifteen hundred dollars in her pocket burned.

Why couldn't Peter do this himself? He was the bold, brave one; she was the timid mouse. And this was even worse for a woman. She didn't even want to think about what could happen. An image flashed before her eyes of the two strangers in her bedroom that night who would have followed Peter's urging if not for her blond defender.

Ooof! Where had that come from? She'd buried that memory two months ago. What was it doing spring up at a time like this? When she was already so scared—so terrified!—she was about to pee her pants and could barely hold back tears that would certainly gush forth if she let loose the dam.

She pushed the memory aside. Buried it back where it belonged. And tried to stop thinking about how this was more dangerous for a woman, and how Peter really hadn't asked, he'd demanded. She'd had no choice. But when did she ever have a choice? Not that she was complaining. Although, she knew she was. She didn't want to be here. Wanted to get out of here as fast as possible.

Guilt washed over her. How could she be so selfish? Peter, her fiancée, the man with whom she was going to spend the rest of her life, was in desperate trouble, and she was complaining about helping him? What was wrong with her? She should *want* to help him. She should be ready to do whatever it took to help him.

Even if she was just a mouse. It was time for this mouse to have a backbone and be there for her man.

But why did she have to be a mouse? Why were her proverbial whiskers always twitching with fear?

Where was the stupid taco truck? And why couldn't it drive to a safer neighborhood? Heck, it was a truck! Why couldn't it do deliveries? Be the Dominoes of tacos! And whatever else "the special" entailed.

Her palms moist, Lizzie squeezed the Hyundai's steering wheel even harder, wondering if it was possible for it to crack and fall apart at the hands of a twig like herself. Wouldn't that be how her luck ran! Have the car break down in this neighborhood even though she serviced it precisely on time, even down to oil changes every three thousand miles.

Get me out of here!

And then suddenly, miraculously, as if in answer to prayer—though she'd stopped believing in such a thing about a decade ago—the form of a white truck appeared in the distance, parked

127

beneath the hazy, orange glow of a sodium streetlight.

Strains of the Hallelujah Chorus played in Lizzie's mind, mocking her to be sure, but she thought she just might get out of this alive.

As she pulled up behind the vehicle, she saw that it was battered and old, maybe even older than she was. At some point in the distant past, the sign on the rear had read JESSE'S TACOS in thick, foot-high black letters against the white background. But the first E and the O were now little more than smudges, making it J SSE'S TAC S.

Who would actually eat at a place like this? The smells in the air of fried beef, chicken, and pork might have their allure for non-vegetarians, not to mention the fried corn tortillas, but what hit her nose hardest was the distinctly unappetizing smell of grease. *Eeew, gross!* Then again, she wasn't here for the food.

Seeing no customers around—no surprise there—and no other lurking threats, Lizzie took a deep breath, patted the money split evenly in her two pants pockets, tried unsuccessfully to calm her pounding heart, and got out of the car.

A huge, middle-aged black man waited for her at the truck's service window, his hands resting on the counter, leaning forward. Lizzie didn't follow sports, but she guessed he might have played for the Bears years ago at one of the positions that hit other players and hit them hard. He had to be six-five or taller, and close to three hundred pounds.

Though the night had turned a bit cold after unseasonably warm days in the sixties and even low seventies, so Lizzie was wearing her navy-blue coat, the hulking form looming over her wore nothing more on his upper half than a sleeveless, white undershirt she'd heard called a wife-beater. Tattoos covered every inch of his massive, heavily muscled arms, and every inch of his neck. There was even a tattoo of a tear leaking from his right eye.

Lizzie gulped. "Are you Jesse?"

"Yeah, I'm Jesse."

Lizzie thought if she ever got a tattoo—which she never, ever would; she felt squeamish just thinking about it, but if she did—that tear tattoo would be right for her. She should have tattoos of hundreds of tears streaming down her face. That would be a Lizzie tattoo.

But maybe Jesse's tear tattoo wasn't supposed to symbolize crying. He looked like he'd never cried once in his life.

"Um, Jesse, I'd like the special."

Jesse's eyes narrowed. When he blinked, Lizzie halfway expected tattoos on the eyelids that said something like K-I-L-L or H-A-T-E.

"What special?" he said, looking at her like she was a bug.

Which was, of course, perfectly reasonable. Lizzie couldn't blame him. She was, after all, just a bug. Nothing more than a cockroach.

She swallowed hard. "The special, special." Her heart jack-hammered.

"*You* want the special, special?" he asked, cocking his head in disbelief. "You?"

"It's for my boyfriend." Lizzie corrected herself. "My fiancée."

Jesse laughed, his entire body rolling with mirth. "Which one? And do your fiancée know about your boyfriend? You don't really seem the type."

Lizzie blinked. What was he saying?

Then she got it.

"Oh," she said. She forced a laugh. "Sorry. I just…"

Lizzie didn't know what to say, so she just let it hang there until she realized this Jesse might actually think she could actually do that, could actually have a fiancée and cheat on him with another man. But of course he did. Even this Jesse, a total stranger who'd known her for less than minute, could sense that she was a depraved woman who, at least if she were more beautiful, could have both a fiancée *and* a boyfriend.

She had no secrets from anyone.

"Oh my goodness, no," Lizzie said quickly. "They're the same. My boyfriend—" Her lips formed the letter P, and she almost blurted out his name, a slip Peter had warned her she better not do or face the most dire of consequences. But she just felt so flustered, her face suddenly feeling hot and sweat beading on her forehead. "I'd never do that."

Jesse snorted. "That's what they all say." He shrugged. "Although you, I probably believe it." He cocked his head again. "Tell me, if you engaged to be married, where's your diamond ring?"

Lizzie felt herself redden. It was back in the apartment, safe in her sock drawer. But could she say that? Could she admit out loud to this man that she hadn't been about to bring something so valuable down to Fuller Park? What would he think of that? It wasn't hard to guess.

She looked quickly all about her, spinning around, checking to make sure no one had snuck up on her and the fifteen hundred dollars that was most surely burning a hole in her pockets.

Jesse chuckled. "Let me guess. White girl like you ain't wearing no diamond ring cause you in Fuller Park. Think all we got here is muggers and thieves and worse. You take it off tonight for the first time since he give it to you. I bet you ain't never even been to Fuller Park before, am I right?"

Lizzie couldn't lie. She could only shake her head no.

"Could I, um, could I just please have the special, Mr., um, Mr. Jesse?" she asked, feeling as though a log had slid down her throat. Then a light went off in her head. "In fact, could I, um, could I get two of them? My boyfriend, I mean, my fiancée, seems"—and she suddenly realized she was talking far too much, just blabbing away, about to say that Peter seemed really afraid and nervous for the first time ever so this had to be really important, just blurting out what she almost certainly was supposed to keep secret—"um, if I could get two, that would be very much appreciated."

Jesse nodded. "Okay, two. But the special-special be a little more expensive tonight than usual. Gonna cost you."

Lizzie nodded rapidly. "Okay."

Jesse called over his shoulder. "A special-special for our special guest here. Two of them." He gave the eye to the tall girl running the fryer. She stood near six feet tall with broad shoulders. Almost certainly his daughter. Jesse turned back to Lizzie. "The special is a chimichanga. Beef or chicken?"

"No, I want the special-special," Lizzie said, confused. How could her intent have been misunderstood? No chimichanga on Earth could protect Peter. "Two special-specials."

Jesse leaned forward. "The special-special comes with the regular special, which tonight is a chimichanga. Beef. Or chicken."

"Oh," Lizzie said, then thought, *eeew!* Deep fried. How awful. Why not just inject the fat directly into the arteries? Although what did she expect at a taco truck, spinach salad and avocado toast?

"Could you make one of them vegetarian?"

Jesse roared with laughter. His tear tattoo danced. "You're getting the special-special—two of 'em—but you want your chimichanga vegetarian. That's a good one. Never got that before."

Lizzie waited. She was used to being laughed at.

Finally, Jesse settled down. "We don't do vegetarian. This is a fucking taco truck." He shook his head. "Excuse my language. Beef or chicken."

"I'm sorry." Lizzie stared down at the ground. "Beef, please, for both." She'd bring them both back to Peter, though they'd need to be reheated. She wasn't hungry.

"Seven each," Jesse said. "Fourteen total."

Ooof! Lizzie recoiled. That was a lot more than she had thought. She barely had enough. Good thing she brought extra. Peter had initially said a couple hundred for one. *Fourteen hundred dollars. Ouch!*

Lizzie couldn't remember ever having a funny thought before

in her life. In fact, she didn't even understand what was funny about most jokes. They went right over her head. But a quip suddenly came to her and she blurted it out.

"These better be *really* good chimichangas."

Her eyes widened, and her hand flew to her mouth as if it could stuff the words back in.

But Jesse laughed. "Close to the best chimichangas we ever had."

Lizzie nodded and looked around. No one there. Out of her right pants pocket, she pulled the first seven hundred and fifty in wrapped twenties sandwiched inside a few tens, and palmed them over to Jesse, feeling like a spy. Then she pulled the identical roll out of her left pocket, removed the hundred in twenties she'd have left, and palmed the rest over to Jesse.

Jesse took the money in his huge hands, and it disappeared beneath the counter.

"I don't usually say this," he said, "but I see you do have a few dollars left. A tip never hurts. Could add an extra guarantee about the quality."

Lizzie wordlessly handed the extra hundred over. As long as she got out of here alive, and whatever she was purchasing kept Peter safe—*these better be really good chimichangas, had she really said that?*—then it was money well spent.

Minutes later, Jesse reappeared and handed her two large brown paper bags like the kind she got at the grocery store, but with the tops rolled up.

"See you next week," he said with a laugh.

Lizzie smiled weakly, her heart still in her throat, knowing he was having fun with her and not minding, just wanting to get back to her car and get out of here.

She locked the car doors as soon as she got in, and quickly drove off without looking at what was in the bags sitting on the passenger seat until she was well out of Fuller Park. The chimichangas smelled quite enticing, but she had no interest in food.

She finally stopped at a brightly lit, all-night Citgo station and convenience store. She didn't need gas. She'd topped the tank off earlier. But she pulled into the bay next to pump seven, well away from any other cars, and cautiously unrolled the top of the bag and opened it.

On top was the chimichanga wrapped in white paper with a big smiley scribbled on top. Beneath it was a dirty white towel. Lizzie tugged at it.

Wrapped inside the towel was a gun and its magazine. She looked closer at the lettering on the slide. Glock 34Gen4 Austria 9x19.

Peter, what have you done?

The instant Peter saw the delicious babe in the slinky, black, fuck-me dress walk into Flirts & Skirts, he knew he had to have her. He had a perfect view as she stood in the arched entranceway. His back was to the wall, the fifty-foot-long bar on his right running all the way to the rear, three deep with those waiting to order. The dance floor diagonally to his right was packed with patrons holding their drinks and moving to the pulsing music.

The smell of sex was in the air. Oh yeah. And Peter was a-sniffing. Perfume and cologne, too, and, of course, alcohol. But mostly sex.

Peter sipped his Jack and Coke, felt the burn, and watched the delicious babe, clutching a small, black purse, avoid dancers and cut toward the bar. Going right across his field of view, only twenty feet away. It was no accident that he had a perfect view. He was no rookie.

Her hips swayed. Her tits jiggled. Long, jet-black hair flowed down her shoulders. Green eyes, perhaps, though it was hard to tell for sure in the club's scant light. Perfect makeup and long lashes.

Possibly a model, although here in Hyde Park she was more likely another UC student. But holy shit, she could be a model.

With just a touch of innocence.

Well, he'd take care of *that*. Oh yeah, he *had* to have this one.

One way or another.

And he *would* have her. Oh, yeah. Every which way but loose. And loose, too.

She was quite obviously alone. No boyfriend or concerned girlfriends to look after her, butting in. Peter smiled. It would be smooth sailing. She had come here to get nailed, and he was going to do the nailing.

Her legs flashed beneath her barely covered ass. Not just any legs. Spread-me-wide-and-pound-me-all-night-long legs. Make-me-walk-bowlegged-in-the-morning legs.

Oh yeah.

Peter moved to his right so their paths would intersect behind the three-deep throng waiting for drinks. When they collided, he turned to his left, saw her, and put a surprised look on his face.

"Sorry," he said, flashing his best smile. "Like sardines in here."

She eyed him warily, sized him up quickly, and clearly liked what she saw. Of course. He was wearing black jeans and a form-fitting dark blue shirt that showed off his physique. And he had great, soft hair that women loved. They all said so.

"Is this really the line to order a drink?" she asked.

"'Fraid so," Peter said. "I figured I'd get in line now with a half-full drink and it'll be gone by the time one of the bartenders gets to me."

"Tell me about it," she said.

"Hey, let me buy you a drink," Peter said, giving the beauty his most dazzling smile. "To make up for that Patrick Kane hip check I accidentally threw at you."

"Patrick who?"

"Patrick Kane. Black Hawks. I guess you're not a hockey fan, or not from here."

"Both."

Peter nodded. "Where you from?"

"Boston."

"Boo!"

Her perfectly trimmed eyebrows shot up. "Excuse me?"

"I've hated all the Boston sports teams since I was little. Hate 'em all."

Her eyes twinkled. "You hate us 'cause you ain't us."

"And here I thought I was falling in love with you."

She looked at him, sizing him up again, with eyes that were, in fact, green. He'd been right. "Slow down there, cowboy."

"Name's Peter."

"Alicia."

She was careful, this Alicia. Peter supposed all hot babes were—they had to be—and maybe plenty that weren't hot at all. They'd been warned about guys like him, so they were careful. Don't drink too much. Don't accept a drink from a stranger. Don't leave your drink unattended. Blah, blah, blah. Careful, careful, careful.

Fucking pains in the asses. But they almost always slipped up. Alicia, too.

On her third Sex on the Beach, she eyed him carefully as he took the drink from the bartender and handed it to her, never taking her eye off it. But Peter hadn't studied magic for five years as a teenager for nothing. She never spotted the roofie he'd removed from his jeans pocket earlier, palmed, and then dropped in her drink as he passed it to her.

He even got fortunate after he took his own drink from the bartender and paid with a handsome tip. A bearded blond guy who had to be six-four and easily two-hundred-forty pounds—a fucking lumberjack dressed in a yellow-checked flannel shirt—bumped into Peter, and then asked if he could dance with Alicia.

"Fuck off!" Peter snapped.

"I believe it should be the lady's decision," the lumberjack said.

Peter glared. He was a good fighter. Had had lots of practice. But he didn't like his odds against this behemoth. "She's not interested." Peter almost added, but only thought, *why would she be interested in you when she can have me?*

Alicia touched his elbow, then spoke to the interloper. "I'm with Peter."

Only after the behemoth lumbered away did Peter realize the distraction had ensured the roofie had dissolved completely. It had been annoying to think the lumberjack was trying to take what was rightfully Peter's, but all's well that ends well.

Peter took a gulp of his Jack and Coke to calm his nerves and waited for Alicia to slip into oblivion. He thought of the many things he would do to her and smiled. Every which way but loose. And then loose, too.

And take photos, of course, for his ever-growing collection.

He hit the Jack and Coke again, then blinked. Alicia was looking at him funny. Or was it that she herself was looking funny?

Blurry?

Peter closed his eyes tightly, then opened them wide. Alicia was just a blur.

He blinked rapidly. The room with its pounding music spun faster and faster.

He tried to say, "What's happening?" but the words came out all jumbled up.

And then everything went black.

Peter awoke early the next morning, lying naked in bed in a strange hotel room. The mother of all hangovers was crushing his skull. His stomach heaved and rolled like a ship pitching up and down on an angry sea. Sunlight streamed through the window, its shades wide open, piercing his eyeballs. His head was splintering apart, piece by piece into tiny sharp slivers. He was Humpty Dumpty, and they'd never put him back together again.

The room smelled of alcohol and sex. His mouth was cotton dry. Past the foot of the queen-sized bed, a TV sat on the right half of a wide laminated surface. Beneath it were empty storage cubes. To the left, a desk chair. The walls were painted with a bright orange shade that made Peter's already queasy stomach churn.

Where the fuck was he? As if in answer, Peter saw the navy-blue sign through the window.

MOTEL 6
WIFI HERE

Motel fucking 6? What the hell was he doing here? This wasn't the hotel he'd checked into last night before heading to Flirts & Skirts.

He rolled out of bed, and instantly regretted it, staggering on weak legs, almost falling flat on his face before realizing that he needed to get to the bathroom fast. He made it just in time, retching his guts out as he worshiped the porcelain god.

What the fuck.

With every bare-assed heaving of his guts, Peter's skull exploded and jagged flashes of lightning crossed his field of vision. *Kill me now.* When he could retch no more and even the dry heaves had mercifully stopped, he spit, grimacing at the sour taste in his mouth, and flushed the toilet for the sixth time.

He put his right arm across the back of the toilet seat and gently rested his Humpty Dumpty of a forehead on it. What the hell had happened?

The last thing he could remember was...

What?

Slowly it came to him. The tasty piece in the black fuck-me dress. What was her name? Couldn't remember. But what difference did that make? He didn't give a flying fuck about any of their names. Other than as a label to go with the pictures.

Pictures. Yeah. Pictures. They'd jar his memory. If he couldn't remember the fun he'd had with...with...with whoever the fuck she was—

Alicia! That was it.

Had he brought her to this dump? Why, when he'd already checked in elsewhere, as usual getting a secluded room near the back? Well, she was gone now if she'd ever been here at all. And he couldn't remember a fucking thing. Which was a pity because she was quite the piece.

The pictures. They'd remind him. Where was the Nikon?

Peter staggered bare-assed back into the room toward the bed—painfully bright orange everywhere—and searched even as the room pitched and heaved around him.

The Nikon was nowhere to be found.

With growing alarm, Peter yanked the covers off the bed. Grabbed his boxers, jeans, and long-sleeved blue shirt off the floor. Tossed them onto the bed. Checked the storage cubes below the TV even though they were empty. Got down on all fours, almost collapsing in the process, and checked beneath the bed.

Searched every square inch.

Nothing.

The bitch had stolen the Nikon! And far more importantly, she had the memory card inside it that held his most prized possessions. Possessions that could not fall into the wrong hands. Peter's pulse pounded painfully in his brain.

Unless.

Unless he'd been so wasted—and he felt totally fucking trashed right now—that he hadn't even managed to get the Nikon out of the Acura's trunk. Had missed the opportunity to capture that bitch Alicia in all her glory. How totally wasted was that?

He sank to the bed and pulled on his clothes, not bothering with shoes and socks. Barefoot, he grabbed his keys and stepped out into the painful sunlight, wincing. Fortunately, the silver

Acura ILX was parked directly in front of the first-floor room, less than ten feet away. He maybe couldn't do a hundred feet, but he could do ten. At least he'd followed that much of the usual plan. With his bare feet cold against first the concrete walkway and then the asphalt of the parking lot, Peter padded to the trunk, popped it with his key fob, and pulled back the carpet-and-cardboard cover atop the spare tire wheel well where he hid his Nikon SLR.

The black, hard-shell case was sitting right there where it was supposed to be. Relief and regret flooded over him simultaneously. Relief that the bitch hadn't stolen the camera and its priceless images after all. Regret that he hadn't captured any of her. How could he have missed an opportunity like that? She had to look glorious naked! And even better after that.

Wondering how he could possibly have been *that* wasted, Peter grabbed the case. His heart sank. It was far too light. He clicked open the latch.

The Nikon wasn't there. The case was empty.

Peter rocked back and forth on unsteady legs. The bitch *had* stolen it!

This couldn't be happening. Ninety-nine percent of the time, he kept it in its usual ultra-safe hiding place where not even the cops could find it. He brought it out only for nights like last night. So he could get the most perfect images possible. His iPhone, the latest model just recently released, was good, but it was no Nikon. And there were some memories that had to be captured in their most exquisite perfection.

But he couldn't afford for the Nikon to fall into the wrong hands. Its cost was the least of his worries. If nothing else, he could get Lizzie, who thought he was on a road trip with some friends to watch the UC football team play an away game, to buy him a new one. No, it was what was on the memory card that concerned him.

He rubbed his eyes, as if somehow that would magically make the Nikon reappear. It didn't. Peter stared at the empty case, then began to frantically search first his gym bag with its change of clothes, the rest of the trunk, and then all the car.

The Nikon was gone.

Mouth dry and still tasting of sour vomit, Peter licked his lips. He sank into the driver's seat, feet hanging out the open door. How could he have let this happen? He was always so careful, archiving the images on USB thumb drives that he encrypted and password protected before hiding. Even if uncovered by the police, they almost certainly couldn't crack his protection.

But thumb drives could go bad all by themselves. They could get ruined by fire or water damage. Or the PC he did the encryption on could fail, rendering the drives unreadable. None of that had happened to him, but he'd read about it.

And he just couldn't take the risk of ever losing those photos. Couldn't take the risk of losing those women. He *owned* them. So just in case, he'd kept the best photos on the Nikon, too, which wasn't as secure. Protecting images on a Nikon meant protecting them from accidental deletion, not from being able to view them on the camera itself.

And now it was in Alicia's hands. Possibly stolen this morning after he'd taken pictures of her last night. Peter ran his fingers through his hair. How could he have fucked up so badly? He'd have to call her and somehow get the camera back. Even if he had to beat it out of her. But he never exchanged numbers during hookups like this. Why make it easy to find him? And if she'd said her last name, he sure as shit couldn't remember it.

Just in case, Peter pulled his iPhone out of his jeans pocket. It had been a fucked-up night. Maybe he had gotten her number. He thumbed the Home button.

He almost dropped the phone.

His head spun. Air rushed out of his lungs. He grabbed hold of the steering wheel to steady himself.

It couldn't be. This just wasn't possible.

But there it was in vivid color. His head propped up against a pillow. Inches away, two erect dicks, one white, one black, dangled over his wide-open mouth.

Peter gagged. He bent over and ducked his head outside the door. His empty stomach heaved. He retched uncontrollably over and over, dry heaving even as his head seemingly split in two.

There was no way he could ever have done that. Never, ever. There wasn't enough alcohol in the world to make him feel anything but total disgust for this.

He checked and saw there was just that one horrific photo. But, of course, one was all it took. *Other than that, Mrs. Lincoln, how did you like the play?*

How had someone unlocked his phone and taken that picture? That impossible, disgusting picture. Had he somehow been incapacitated and someone pressed his thumb to the Home button and unlocked the phone? How could—

Incapacitated.

Peter's panicked, fractured mind finally slipped the pieces into place. He figured out what should have been obvious to him soon after he woke up. He'd just been too wasted to see it.

That Alicia bitch had set him up. Set him up like a motherfucker.

She had roofied *him!*

Peter picked up his venti caramel macchiato with two extra shots of espresso and collapsed into a chair at a two-person table in the rear of the L-shaped Starbucks. The front tables along the floor-to-ceiling windows were mostly filled with customers noisily chatting and tapping away on laptops. Here in the rear, he was as far away from them as possible, his back turned to them, and he was shielded from the bright sunlight streaming in.

He set the drink down on the circular light-brown tabletop, took off the cup's cover to let the steaming-hot liquid cool, and rubbed his eyes. On another day, he'd enjoy the smell of the steamed milk and espresso along with the vanilla syrup.

Not today.

At the Motel 6, he'd taken a long, hot shower, and changed into the clean clothes he'd packed for the fictitious UC football team road trip: jeans and a long-sleeved, pullover Bears T-shirt of navy blue and burnt orange. But he still felt like shit. He still couldn't believe what his eyes had told him. What his lying eyes had told him.

Now, he needed to think. Even if his brain wasn't cooperating. What the fuck had actually happened? And what the hell was he going to do about it?

He blew on the drink and ventured a sip, getting more caramel drizzle than coffee. It was still too hot, but he needed the caffeine so he took another small sip. Did it really matter at this point if he burned his mouth to a fucking crisp?

"Hey, buddy, how's it hanging?"

The blond, bearded lumberjack from last night slapped Peter on the back and sat down, dropping two large manila envelopes on the table. They landed heavily with an ominous, loud thwack. The huge lumberjack again wore a checked flannel shirt, its golden yellow matching his hair and beard.

"Who the fuck are you?" Peter asked. "What are you doing here?"

The lumberjack leaned close, his thick forearms on the table, and grinned. "I'm your worst fucking nightmare."

A few pieces to the sickening puzzle clicked into place, but not all of them. The lumberjack, who had to be at least six-four, and two-hundred-forty, rock-hard pounds, had been at Flirts & Skirts, trying to home in on Alicia. So how did he fit in?

Peter put the cover back onto the cup and sipped the still-too-hot macchiato, burning his mouth but not showing it, projecting only nonchalance. He had to stay cool. Never let the other asshole even *think* he's getting the upper hand. Even if you've got the equivalent of seven-deuce off-suit, act like you've got aces. But his heart raced.

Peter took another sip. His eyes bored in on the blond lumberjack's cold blue eyes. Again, Peter asked, "Who the fuck are you?"

"You can call me Sven," the lumberjack said. "That's not my real name. Any more than Alicia is my partner's real name. But close enough."

Partner? The word punched Peter in the gut. Things were as bad as he'd feared. Worse. He sank back in his seat, suddenly nauseous. *Your worst fucking nightmare.*

"Partners?" Peter finally managed to ask. "You're like, a couple?"

Sven, the lumberjack, shook his head. "Purely business."

"What do you want?"

Sven smiled. "Everything."

"What do you mean?"

He tapped the two manila envelopes. "We own you, motherfucker."

Peter tried to calm his racing heart and clear the thoughts clanging about inside his brain like a pinball. He'd known his life had turned to pure hell as soon as he'd seen the empty Nikon case and the picture on his phone hours ago, but it was a far hotter hell than he'd imagined.

Steadying his trembling hands, Peter spread his arms wide. "Whatever you think you got on me, I don't have any money."

Sven gave Peter a shooing-away motion.

"You rich boys always cry poor," Sven said. "But you live in a nice apartment, you drive a fancy car, you're wearing designer jeans and Nikes, which each cost a couple hundred dollars, and you're here drinking a six-dollar cup of coffee. Spare me the bullshit. You got money coming out of your ass."

"Honest to God, I'm broke," Peter said. "It's my bitch that has the money. She pays for everything. The apartment. The car. The clothes. Everything." He stopped himself before he added that Lizzie had even paid for her own engagement ring. No need for this prick to know about *that.* "She even puts money on my Starbucks card. That's how I paid for this six-dollar coffee, which thanks to you now tastes like shit."

"Sounds like she's your meal ticket."

"You could say that," Peter said. "But I can't exactly ask her to pay for this...this thing you think you have on me."

"Then I guess you better not let her find out what you've been doing." Again, Sven tapped the envelopes. "Otherwise, your meal ticket goes bye-bye. In fact, she might be the first person we send high-res copies of the photos so she can see every last detail. Before, of course, we paper the walls of UC with them." He slid the top envelope to Peter. "Check it out."

Peter froze.

Sven reached over and slipped the top two photographs out of the envelope. One showed Peter lying on his back. The other showed him on all fours. In both he was naked. Both with two men, one white, one black.

"Got a couple hundred different shots in here," Sven said. "Want to see them?"

The room spun. Peter felt himself about to black out.

"Put those away," he somehow managed to say. "Put them away!"

Sven slid them back in the envelope.

Peter gripped the table to steady himself.

"That isn't me! I'm not—!" He couldn't even say the word. "Not even close!"

"These pictures would argue otherwise. And the one on your phone."

"But I'm not! Never once! That shit disgusts me. I don't know what you did, but that isn't me. You doctored those photos! I would never—"

"Oh, you were quite cooperative," Sven said, beaming. "We didn't have to use your thumbprint to unlock your phone. You were quite happy to tell us your password. All your passwords. Where your car was parked in the Flirts & Skirts parking lot. You handed the keys right over. Oh, you were quite chatty with Alicia. Though not so much with the two guys."

Peter felt his face grow hot and his stomach wretch.

"They didn't really do anything to me, did they?" he said, trying to keep the begging out of his voice. "It was all just staged. Faked. Right?"

Sven shrugged. "I don't know. You tell me. How's your asshole feel?"

Peter lunged across the table but stopped himself halfway. He wanted to rip the guy's heart out of his chest and devour the bloody organ, bite by bite, bit by bit. He wanted to kill the motherfucker. Rip his goddamned smiling face off. Tear that blond beard out by the roots. Wanted to make him suffer.

But not only could the lumberjack tear him in two, the piece of shit also had him by the balls.

Peter sank back in his chair, suddenly short of breath. He looked over his shoulder. No one from the front of Starbucks had noticed.

"Good for you that you didn't touch me," Sven said. "That would have driven up the price. A lot."

"I got no money. What do you want me to do?"

"Then you'll work it off."

"What does that mean?"

"If all else fails, you're a nice piece of ass." Sven smiled grimly. An icy hardness filled his eyes. "And I'm not talking servicing the cougars of Chicago. Your photos from last night could be advertisements. Young, supple flesh. Submissive. We could sell you to enterprises that specialize in that sort of thing."

Peter thought he might vomit all over the table. There wasn't much left in his stomach to puke up, but it was still a struggle to hold down whatever was there. He tried to calm his heaving gut. Clenched his eyes. Sucked in a deep breath. Listened to the jackhammering of his heart and tried to slow the beat.

Slowly. Slowly. Slowly.

Finally, he opened his eyes. The nightmare was still sitting across from him, of course, huge arms crossed, looking down on him as if he were just a bug.

"You've ruined my life!" Peter said through clenched teeth.

"Why? Why me?"

"I think you know."

"No, I don't! Why couldn't you have picked some...some *bisexual* freak who wouldn't care. Why me?" Peter shuddered.

"It's about giving you what you deserve, Peter."

Peter recoiled at the familiar use of his name. Of course, the man knew his identity. He'd been through his wallet. He'd...he'd...Peter tried to push it all from his mind but couldn't.

You tell me. How's your asshole feel?

Please God, Peter thought, let it all have been staged. I'll go to Mass every Sunday for the rest of my life if it was just staged. They couldn't possibly have really...really...

He squirmed in his seat, not really sure how his asshole felt.

"Why me?" he asked again.

"Alicia selected you," Sven said. "She always picks the target. She's good at it. She seems to know which guys are going to try to do what you tried. She has an instinct for that sort of thing. Lots of experience, I guess. Plus in your case, it was easy. A while back, you tried something on a friend of a friend of a friend."

"What do you mean?"

"Don't play dumb. We know."

"I was just—"

"We've got your Nikon. We know." Sven slid the top manila envelope aside and tapped the bottom one. "I could show you these photos, but they won't shock you at all. You already know them by heart. In fact, they really make our photos irrelevant. These are much better for our purposes."

Peter's life, already pushed off a cliff and plummeting to the jagged rocks far below, crash-landed, exploding into bits of dust.

"You were going to do to Alicia the same thing you did to all those girls on the camera," Sven said. "Roofie her. Take her to a remote room at the back of some motor lodge, carry her inside, and take your pictures. Of you pulling her clothes off. Then raping her as she lay there helpless, either unconscious or incoherent. Incapacitated one way or another. No other word for it.

Rape."

Peter looked over his shoulder to make sure no one had gotten close enough to hear.

"I don't know what you're talking about," he said, unable to come up with anything more original than that oldest, lamest line in the book. "I don't even own a Nikon."

Sven smiled. "Not anymore."

All the air went out of Peter's lungs.

"If the police get those pictures," Sven said, "you'll be taking it up the ass in jail from guys even bigger than me. Hard, hard time. Especially for a cute guy like you." Sven nodded. "Real hard time, motherfucker."

Peter couldn't speak for what felt like an eternity. And Sven sat there smugly, letting it all sink in.

"How did Alicia do it?" Peter finally asked, although he thought he'd figured it out.

"She caught you spiking her drink," Sven said, his blue eyes cold and merciless. "We only do this to scumbags like you. We have no innocent victims. Only scumbags who deserve what's coming to them."

"But I didn't—"

Sven cut him off with a wave of his thick hand.

"You were pretty good palming the roofie, but nothing gets past Alicia. Not anymore. You'd have to be Penn and fucking Teller to fool Alicia. So she gave me the eye. Set the wheels in motion. I distracted you so she could drop a roofie in *your* drink. Lights out, Chicago."

"That fucking bitch!" Peter muttered.

"Nah, you know what's the bitch? Payback is the fucking bitch."

Peter glanced over his shoulder to again make sure no one was listening. "So this is like some fucking crusade for you two?"

"It is for Alicia," Sven said. "It's a holy war she's been fighting ever since a piece of shit succeeded doing to her what you just tried. She was a bit naïve back then. Not anymore. So she'd do this for free. Just for the street justice. But me? It ain't no holy war for me. Just a business. Sure beats working for a living. And the pay is *phenomenal.*"

"Let me talk to Alicia," Peter said, taking the longest of long shots. He'd always been able to sweet-talk women. "I could explain."

"How are you going to explain?" Sven asked, shaking his head in disbelief. "With most of the rapist-wannabes, we just have them spiking her drink, and that's all she needs. But with you, we've got the camera, too. Pictures of you assaulting all those girls you roofied. You're not just a wannabe; you've succeeded over and over. We got you red-handed. Not even the ghost of Johnnie Cochran could get you acquitted with Alicia.

"Besides, she's out of the picture now. She doesn't like this part of the business. Gets a little squeamish at the dirty stuff. Doesn't want to know anything about it. Like they say about sausage. She doesn't want to know how the messy sausage of justice is made. She only wants to eat it. And we sure as shit are gonna make sausage out of you." Sven smiled wolfishly. "Alicia just takes her cut and lets the knowledge of getting some street justice try to heal that broken part of her soul. Least that's what she says. '*That broken part of my soul.*' Kinda poetic, I think. Don't you?"

Peter said nothing.

"So you'll never see her again," Sven said. "Unless, of course, you see her at another club sometime, hunting for predators like you. But probably not. We move around. As you might guess, we've got a few enemies. Can't stay in any one place for long."

Beneath the table, Peter clenched and unclenched his fists. His balls were in a vice and the fucking lumberjack was turning the crank. Enjoying himself. Knowing he didn't want to hear the answer, Peter asked the million-dollar question.

"How much are we talking about?"

He almost fell off his chair when he heard it.

"Five thousand for most guys, but not for you. We're not

talking about just the embarrassment some creep feels about pictures like these getting out or getting into the hands of a wife. We're talking felonies. Lifetime in prison without parole felonies. The Nikon changes everything."

"How much?"

"For you, a hundred thousand for everything. You get all the photos, the originals, and the Nikon."

Peter's jaw dropped. "You can't be serious!" He didn't bother to ask how there could be any guarantee that copies hadn't already been made for future blackmailing purposes. He was no fool. They most certainly had. That didn't matter.

A hundred thousand!

"I'd be lucky if I could pay a grand."

"We do have an installment plan," Sven said, smiling.

Peter just stared, struggling to comprehend all of what he'd just heard.

His life was over.

Sven slid the top manila envelope to him. The one with the sickening pictures of him and the two men. "Take these. We don't need them." He tapped the other envelope. "This is all that matters now."

Peter pushed the envelope back. He didn't even want to touch it. "I don't want these."

"Fine," Sven said. "I'll leave them out front on a table by the cash register."

Peter grabbed the envelope back even as it made his skin crawl. "You fucking asshole! Both of you!"

Sven took a phone out of his pants pocket and slid it to Peter. A burner.

"Use this to text or call me. Only me, no one else. My number is in there. Don't say words like 'money' or 'photographs' or the always popular, 'you fucking cocksucker'. You never know who's listening. Use code names like 'delivery' and 'package'. If you don't contact me in forty-eight hours to arrange at least a down payment of five thousand dollars, I'll send your Nikon and this second envelope to the police and tell them where to find you. I can only imagine the price of your bail."

"I can't pay," Peter said.

"Then next time we meet, give yourself an enema first. Clean yourself out. And bring plenty of lube."

The smell of the chimichangas filled the Hyundai, but Lizzie wasn't even tempted. All she could do as she sat parked beneath the brightly lit canopy of the Citgo station was stare at the two paper bags. Stare and wonder, *Peter, what have you done?*

She'd peeked in the second bag, too, and its contents were identical to the first. A chimichanga wrapped in white paper with a smiley on top, no longer hot but not yet cold, and beneath it, the same model Glock and its magazine wrapped inside a dirty white towel.

She couldn't imagine what trouble Peter was in to need a gun. And not just any gun. A gun secretly purchased with cash slipped furtively to a guy in, of all places, a taco truck, and dispensed in a brown paper bag tucked beneath a chimichanga.

An untraceable gun. A bootleg gun that could be used and gotten rid of, even if two of them cost *fourteen hundred dollars* (plus tip). Gotten rid of because it had been used in a crime. If not murder, then at least threatening it.

Peter what have you done? What are you planning to do?

His words came back to her. *It's better that you don't know.* He was probably right about that. But she let that same logic guide her own decision about the second gun. It might be best if Peter didn't know she had it. She couldn't imagine actually committing a crime (other than buying an illegal gun, of course). But she could watch out for him. Be his backup—the one nobody saw coming—and make sure nothing went wrong.

Of course, something was about to go wrong and she knew it. But what could Peter do with a second gun? Firing two guns a-blazing was something that happened only in old Westerns.

Better that she be able to ride to his rescue, or at least try to, if things did run amuck.

She would be his insurance policy.

She could handle a gun. Her father had taken her to a shooting range several times when she was sixteen after their house had been broken into. But she hadn't liked it. Especially after she found herself pretending the target was Uncle Bob. And then her mother. And finally herself.

Ooof!

Lizzie shook herself like a dog coming out of water. She'd made her decision and that was that. She wouldn't tell Peter because, in his own words, *it's better you don't know.* He'd probably get it out of her. He'd even gotten her to tell him about Julie. When it came to loose lips sinking ships, her ship might as well be already at the bottom of the ocean.

But she could at least try. She'd protect her future husband, no matter who was threatening him.

Lizzie rolled the nearest bag up tight, got out of the car, and put the bag in the trunk in the spare wheel well, then covered it with a pile of blankets.

She would stand by her man.

Where is she? Where is that stupid bitch? Peter paced back and forth inside the apartment. *How long does it take to drive to Fuller Park and back?*

The fleeting thought occurred to him that Lizzie might have gotten hurt or killed or at least robbed. If so, he was fucked. He had no contingency plan for a gun beyond the taco truck. He was counting on the silly twit, God help him.

Peter froze when the key turned in the lock, then he all but tackled her when Lizzie stepped inside the apartment. She started to take off her coat and say something, but he had no time for that shit.

"Let me see it," Peter said, snatching the bag from Lizzie's hand and taking a peek inside. He fumbled past the wrapping of some warm tortilla-like thing, then felt the reassuring outline of a pistol inside the towel. *Yes!* He wanted to take it out and examine every microscopic detail, touch the cold metal, and smell the gun oil. But there was business to take care of first. He narrowed his eyes. "Did you look inside? Don't lie to me!"

Lizzie went all doe-eyed and meek. "You never said I couldn't."

"I must have! And if I didn't, I shouldn't have had to! For fuck's sake, you're a 4.0 in pre-med. Do I have to spell everything out for you?"

"Peter, all you said was to take a thousand dollars into Fuller Park and find a taco truck. I did what you said."

"Are you giving me an attitude?"

"No."

"You better not or you'll be taking your exams next week standing up!"

Lizzie just blinked.

"I'm serious!" he said, then remembered he needed her to pony up more cash. To make the setup look legit. "Hey, I'm sorry." He stroked her cheek. "I'm obviously under a lot of stress." He forced a smile. "Well, since you've already stuck your nose into it"—he shook his head—"let's take a look."

He slid the contents of the bag onto the kitchen table, tossed the wrapper with the tortilla or whatever the fuck it was at the sink and missed—it hung on the edge of the counter—and unwrapped the gun.

"*Oooh!*" Peter said, a warm sensation filling his gut as he slid the web of his hand into the grip and touched his finger to the trigger. "A Glock 34 Gen 4. *Nice!* And in mint condition." He popped the magazine in, popped it out, racked the slide, then popped the magazine back in. He eyed the gun from end to end, holding it up under the ceiling light to see it better. "I was afraid I might get something last used by Wild Bill Hickok. You never know with a place like that."

"Peter, what's happened to you? What's wrong?" Lizzie asked, the sound of her pleading voice taking the edge off the thrill of holding the gun.

"Like I told you before," Peter said between clenched teeth, "it's best you don't know. What you don't know can't hurt you. That's why I didn't want you to open the fucking bag." He waved the Glock. "Didn't want you to see this."

Peter wondered if by some miracle his entire plan did work, would he have to kill Lizzie to leave no loose ends behind? It would tidy things up for sure, but the cops always looked for the boyfriend first. Always. So he could forget that idea. Besides, controlling Lizzie was *never* a problem. If he couldn't keep her silly yap shut, he'd point the gun at his own head and pull the trigger.

"I'm scared," Lizzie said. "I was scared to death in Fuller Park! But even more, I'm scared for you. For whatever must be happening to you. I love you! I want to help."

"Yeah, yeah. I bet it was scary," Peter said, nodding. "Hey, how much is left of the thousand?"

Lizzie looked like she was going to cry. "Nothing."

"*Nothing?* There's nothing left?"

Lizzie shook her head, wide-eyed.

"That bastard charged you a grand?" Peter shook his head, then reconsidered. The Glock 34 Gen 4 was a fine piece of machinery. Most importantly, there was no paper trail. Plus, it was just Lizzie's money. What did he care? But shit, a thousand?

"Listen, I'm going to need another grand," he said. "How soon can you get it?"

"*Another* thousand dollars?" Lizzie cried. "Peter, I've got almost no more money left."

He wanted to slap her. But he counted to three. Once, twice, and then a third time. He took a deep breath. If he made it out of all of this alive, the bitch would be in for more pain than she ever imagined.

"I can't explain it to you," he said in as even a tone as he

153

could manage. "It wouldn't be safe. But I only need the money for an hour and then I'll give it back. I need it for show. I hate to deplete your *fucking* bank account, but this is to save my life."

Lizzie nodded eagerly. "Of course."

"And I'm going to need to use your car. I'm not sure the time yet, but probably nine o'clock or later. A nice car like the Acura is too memorable." He smiled, trying to be charming, though he doubted that he needed to bother. "Your bucket-of-bolts old Hyundai is just what I need."

"Okay."

"Now go get some sleep and forget everything you've seen or heard the last few hours. They didn't happen. Got that? Never happened."

Lizzie nodded so eagerly she looked like a fucking bobblehead doll.

"If I'm not here for dinner, leave the money and your car keys under my pillow. Make sure they're there no later than six o'clock. Then clear out. Go to the library or somewhere. I don't want to see you."

Lizzie put her hand up timidly, like a fucking fifth-grader asking the teacher to speak.

"What?" Peter snapped.

"Can't I do anything to help?"

"You can help me by getting the fucking money and then getting out of the fucking way. I don't want you distracting me. And it's best you don't see a fucking thing. Understood?"

With the sniveling bitch out of the way and soon snoring loudly— if only he could get away with taking a pillow, clamping it down hard over her fucking mouth, and silencing her forever!—Peter closed the bedroom door and moved to the picture window overlooking the street. Below there was only darkness, broken by the orange glow of streetlamps and the headlights of the occasional car.

It was now past two in the morning. Probably too late to call or text the asshole, but he might still be up.

Peter typed into the burner, *We need to talk.*

The phone rang. Peter answered.

"Do you realize what time it is?" Sven asked.

"Am I interrupting your beauty sleep?"

"Not at all. I'd just think you wouldn't want to piss me off."

"Like you could make things any worse for me?"

Sven snickered. "Don't tempt me."

"We need to talk."

"We're talking."

"In person."

"Not happening. Either you make your delivery or I make mine."

"I can't do it, but I've got an offer you might be interested in."

"You seem to think I'm willing to negotiate."

"I can make a partial delivery and make up for the shortfall."

"How?"

"We need to meet in person. Even burners can be eavesdropped on. And I need to show you my offer. Make my presentation. Plus, of course, make the partial delivery."

"How much of a partial delivery?"

"One. I know it ain't five, but it's a good-faith partial. And you'll be interested in what I've got to show you. I guarantee it."

Sven went silent. Peter held his breath. This was just one of the many pieces that had to come together to even give him a chance. He had to be right about all his guesses, and a lot of luck had to go his way. Even then, he'd still be a long shot to come out of it alive. But if this first piece to the puzzle didn't happen, he didn't have a chance.

"When?" Sven finally said.

"I'm getting the partial during the day tomorrow. So anytime tomorrow night. You pick the time and place."

"Nine o'clock. Get in your car then and start driving. I'll call you and tell you where to go."

Lizzie hatched the plan in her free hour between Biochemistry and Cell Biology. It took her seventeen minutes because it wasn't a good plan. It was preposterous to think it could somehow work—it only put her in a position to help Peter, nothing more—and almost everything could go wrong. But it was the best she could do.

The idea came to her during the first of the seventeen minutes because, of course, it was obvious considering where she'd left the Glock. *Her* Glock, as she now thought of it. Sixteen minutes later, she hadn't thought of anything else. Creativity was not her strong suit. In truth, it wasn't a suit at all. She would have kept trying—she would try forever for Peter—but she theorized that perhaps her subconscious could do better so she switched to her studies for the other forty-three minutes. But even her subconscious came up empty.

So after leaving her car keys and the money under the pillow as commanded—this thousand dollars had required a cash advance on her MasterCard because the checking account had truly been sucked dry—Lizzie slipped outside to her Hyundai, which she'd left unlocked minutes before. She popped the trunk, locked the doors, and after checking to make sure that no one was watching, climbed into the trunk, legs on the driver's side, and pulled it shut. Shifting to lay on her left side, she snuggled beneath the three thick woolen blankets she'd brought down earlier along with a warm coat, just in case, and hunkered down in the darkness for what might be a long wait.

She'd done her homework. Lizzie Hosker always did her homework. These were cramped quarters, to be sure, no matter how tiny she was. Her knees were bent so they came halfway up to her chest. But she'd manage. She certainly wasn't claustrophobic, not after the various hoods and other paraphernalia that Peter employed. And there was no danger of becoming locked in the trunk. The Hyundai, as did all cars since the turn of the century, came with an internal trunk release that required a mere flick of a glowing orange knob to open it. The trunk was far from air-tight. She wouldn't suffocate. The blankets and coat would keep her warm even if the late-night air turned cold. She'd drank no liquids since this morning, and she'd peed just before she came down.

Beneath the covers were the three things she thought needed: a tiny flashlight no larger than an AA battery, her phone set to silent mode, and the Glock. As prepared as possible.

In the end, though, she wasn't prepared at all.

Peter had been driving the Hyundai in random directions, cursing with every right and left he took, for twenty minutes before he got the call on the burner. He'd hidden the Glock in the underside of the dashboard, duct-taping it with just a single thin strip to the back of the paneling where the paneling ended and the steering column extended to the front-end assembly. His tiny bottle of pepper spray, so small he could palm it undetected, was nestled in a "magician's" sleeve sewn into the underside of his shirt at the right elbow.

He knew he was a prohibitive long shot. His guesses needed to be correct, and plenty of luck had to fall his way. Even with all that, he'd still probably fail.

But he was going down with all guns blazing. Fucking Lizzie and her kind would just roll over and take it, but not him. No way was he going to jail. No way was he going to pay a blackmailer, especially since copies had been made of everything. He'd be forever under the thumb of that shithead Sven, powerless to wriggle free. Peter wasn't about to pay forever in cash or services of any kind, whether it be selling his ass—no fucking way!—or muling drugs or anything.

If he could actually cash in a life insurance policy on himself, he'd buy a big one right now because a long life culminating in a quiet retirement was not in the cards. Odds had to be a million-to-one against him being alive a year from now. Hell, a month from now. For fuck's sake, maybe even a day from now. He was holding a shitty hand and Sven held aces. But Peter was ready to crack those aces into tiny little pieces. And if he didn't? Better a bullet in the head than a dick up his ass. Even a metaphorical one.

So when Sven's circuitous directions led Peter to a deserted street in a rundown area with boarded-up triple-decker houses on the right and a football-field-sized vacant lot on the left, he pulled to the curb alongside the triple-deckers, well aware that his body might soon be lying in the lot across the street. But with a shit-ton of luck, the body would instead be Sven's.

"Pull underneath the streetlamp, turn on the interior overhead light, and turn off the car," Sven dictated over the burner phone. "Put the cash on the passenger seat next to you. Then put your hands in the air and touch the ceiling."

Peter followed the orders even though no other car, and no other person, was in sight.

"No sudden movements or you're a dead man," Sven said. "Put the phone on speaker, roll down the window, and put the phone on the roof."

Peter did as instructed.

"Slowly, and I mean slowly or it'll be the last fucking thing you do," came the command over the speaker phone from the roof, "slowly reach through the window, use the handle to open the door, and with your hands up, slowly get out."

Peter grimly did so. *Good-bye Glock.*

"Hands against the hood. Spread your legs."

Peter complied, even as the cold air rippled through his shirt and chilled his skin.

A black SUV skidded to a stop behind the Hyundai, high beams supplemented by blinding floodlights. Car doors opened.

Peter's heart sank even further. Two car doors had opened, one right after another. It had been a long shot, but he had hoped he would be going up against Sven *mano a mano*. The huge blond had approached him alone in Starbucks and had then talked almost exclusively about him and Alicia. He'd then said that Alicia got squeamish at the dirty side of the business, so she left that to him. She wanted to eat the sausage without knowing how it was made.

Eat my sausage, you fucking bitch! Peter thought, then tried to calm back down. He had to think straight. Be cool.

So no Alicia. Sven had also made it seem as though it was just a two-person operation, him and Alicia. Whoever the two men were who had at least pretended to rape him in the pictures—had they actually...penetrated him? Peter wasn't sure he wanted to know—it sounded like they were just a couple of fucking perverts who did what they did for free. For the fucking fun of it. Or else they were hired hands, locals that didn't travel with Sven and Alicia as they crisscrossed the country in their campaign of harsh street justice. An especially likely possibility if his "scenes" had just been staged, and not the real thing. Just local actors with a sick fucking sense of humor.

But Peter knew now his assumption—or had it been wishful thinking?—that he was only against the two ringleaders, one of whom didn't like the dirty stuff, was false.

Someone else was back there with Sven. Maybe one of the actors—please God, Peter hoped, let them be actors and not perverts—but maybe this was an even larger operation and the extra was a bodyguard. Or a hit man.

So much for having even a long shot of a chance.

Footfalls crunched briefly on the potholed asphalt, sounding like one from each side of the SUV, then stopped, maintaining a safe distance out of range of the pepper spray. If Peter could even get at it without getting shot first.

Peter glanced back, but, blinded by the harsh floodlights mounted atop the SUV, he could only make out two vague shapes dressed all in black, including black ski masks covering their faces. Sven's huge shape from the driver's side and a short guy on the

David H. Hendrickson

other. Just the two vague shapes and the glint of steel. Pistols.

"Hands up!" yelled Sven from the driver's side. "Turn and face the front of your car! Your back to me!"

Peter had hoped that the smug, cavalier prick who'd approached him alone in Starbucks would be arrogant enough—or shorthanded enough if the perverts weren't really part of the picture—to either make some kind of mistake or give Peter some opening. But the prick wasn't alone and he hadn't made a single mistake.

"What the fuck is up with the change of cars?" Sven demanded. "Where's the Acura? I ought to shoot you right now!"

"Relax," Peter said. "It's an old piece of shit. I figured you're probably gonna kill me anyway no matter what I do. Why ruin a nice car if you're going to fill it with bullet holes?"

"You trying to be a wise guy?"

"No, I just like that Acura. And thought it might catch attention. It's a nice car. I didn't know you'd be bringing me someplace like this."

"Try anything funny and it's your fucking funeral."

"I got it. I ain't gonna try anything funny."

Silence hung in the air for a long time. Peter wondered if Sven and his accomplice were sending each other hand signals or something.

"Cash is on the passenger seat?" Sven finally asked.

"Yes."

"Okay, turn your back to the cash. Face the other side of the street. Face the vacant lot you're gonna get buried in if you try anything funny."

Gravel crunched, then behind Peter, the Hyundai's passenger door opened. A rustling sound came from the seat, presumably the cash being stuffed in a bag.

"So what's your business proposal?" Sven asked.

"Can I put my hands down?" Peter asked, his right hip against the open door, still blinded by the radiant floodlight.

"No!"

160

Sven, still masked, remained twenty feet away, his pistol trained on Peter. The short guy was presumably on the other side of the Hyundai, his sights aimed at the back of Peter's head.

Two guns vs. none. *Say good-night, Peter boy.*

Other than the last card he still had left to play, his pathetic excuse for a proposal had boiled down to "lure you here with a thousand bucks, then try to get you to make a mistake." A piece-of-shit plan, to be sure, one that Sven had shredded to pieces, but it wasn't as though Peter had been able to enlist Little Miss Four-point-fucking-oh to come up with anything better. The bitch was useless for anything like this. Useless for almost anything except this last card.

A wild card. Time to play it.

"The woman I live with," Peter said, "I've bled her dry. She said there's nothing left and I believe her. And like I told you before, I ain't got any money myself. Now you can talk all you want about selling my ass on the streets, but I hate queers. I'll either kill someone or kill myself. I'm not a valuable commodity.

"But the woman is another story. She'll take it. She's been taking it all her life. She'll take it forever. You, or someone you sell her to, can make a mint off her if you do it right. She can be a fucking gold mine.

"She's no beauty. Kind of a Plain Jane type. Tiny, barely five feet tall. Almost no tits at all. But you can use that to your advantage. A while back I got her to shave her pussy. She looks like she's only twelve years old.

"Put her in pigtails and a Catholic schoolgirl dress, and she'll be the dream of every kiddie fiddler in Chicago. Detroit. New York City. Wherever. And she takes a whipping. Oh yeah, she can take a hellacious whipping. I can show you pictures and everything. Got 'em on my phone right here.

"So let's deal. My ass for hers. She's got no living family. No friends at all. I'm all she's got. I'll cover with the school. I'll come up with something, and no one will even know that she's gone. Ain't no one will give a shit. Trust me. Let me show you the pictures! I got 'em right here."

When the car had started moving, Lizzie's heart skipped a beat. Finally! She wasn't sure if it was a good thing or a bad thing, but they were moving. The rubber smell of the spare tire filled the trunk's cold, close air. Lizzie listened in vain for Peter's voice—she needed to hear his voice!—as she lay there beneath the blankets, legs cramping, eyes wide, her hands inches from the gun. They seemed to be driving around in what seemed like aimless fashion, making the same uncomfortable turns one after another.

Then the phone rang and she heard Peter's reassuring voice. At first just specifying what street they were on, and then a lot of "okay" and "yes" reactions to commands she couldn't hear.

But it was good to hear his voice. Lizzie exhaled in relief. Her racing heart calmed ever so slightly.

Until the car stopped.

Lizzie sucked in a gulp of air. Her hand gripped the Glock. Her heart jackhammered. Then he began to talk about her.

"The woman I live with, I've bled her dry," Peter said.

No, Peter!

But it got worse. So much worse.

As he continued on, she had all she could do not to cry out in pain. A pain far worse than all his most extreme punishments.

Her heart broke into tiny little shards.

When he completed his proposal—"My ass for hers...Ain't no one will give a shit"—Lizzie's heart ceased to exist.

"That's not a proposal Alicia will go for," Sven said with what sounded to Peter like an odd, almost comical tone in his voice. "You know she's in this gig because of what happened to her. So when you tried to roofie her, she had no sympathy for you. How's she going to okay a trade of you, someone who was going to rape her, for the innocent woman you live with?"

"Fuck Alicia!" Peter said, gaining hope that he might actually be getting through to Sven, actually had a chance. He might pull the rabbit out of the hat after all. "Alicia doesn't have to know. This can be your deal. Just between you and me. Cut in Shorty, the guy behind me, if you want, or keep all the money yourself. Fuck her and the horse she rode in on."

"Hey, asshole," came a female voice from the other side of the car. "I'm not into horses."

It took a moment for the voice to register. And then...

Aw, fuck. It was Alicia.

Peter closed his eyes and took a deep breath. Resigned, he said to Sven, "I thought you said she doesn't like the dirty work." He gestured over his shoulder toward Alicia. "What the hell is she doing here?"

"I'm making an exception for you, you asshole," Alicia said. "I'm making an exception for a guy who likes raping incapacitated women so much he has to take photos as mementos of the cherished events. Those photos are going to land you in jail, motherfucker, because this thousand dollars is all we're gonna take from you. 'Cause your Nikon is going to the cops as soon as we leave here so you can rot in jail for the rest of your miserable fucking existence."

Lizzie lay in the trunk unable to move. She had gone from hurt to crushed to...

Destroyed.

This was the man she was going to marry? This monster? Had he ever loved her? Of course, he hadn't. She was unlovable. No wonder he...no wonder he...

She had to ask him if he had *ever* cared for her at all.

Lizzie hit the glowing orange knob. The trunk hood popped up.

* * *

Peter heard a noise from the back of the car and didn't think twice. He wasn't going to get a better opportunity.

He dove onto the front seat, legs dangling out the door, and reached for the Glock strapped to the back of the underpanel. In his peripheral vision, he saw Alicia, off to the right and no longer wearing a ski mask, swing her gun to face the rear of the car.

From behind on his side, a shot boomed.

Peter's knee exploded. Pain tore through him. He screamed. Streaks flashed across his eyes. *Motherfucker!*

But primal instinct kept him moving. Peter tore the gun free from the underpanel. Racking the slide, he rolled onto his back. Sat half-up.

The trunk had somehow popped up, leaving only a small opening in the top right corner of the rear window where he could see Sven's huge frame.

Peter fired. The shot pinged off metal. He fired again. *Ping!* And fired again.

Sven dropped.

What a shot!

But not done yet!

Ears ringing and knee screaming, Peter rolled onto his stomach. Swung his arms to aim the Glock at where Alicia—

She chopped the butt of her gun down on his hands. The Glock clattered uselessly to the dark-carpeted floor near her open door.

More than two feet away.

Peter tried to dive for it, even as his brain screamed in pain. But he got no leverage. He barely moved.

Alicia pounced, grabbed the Glock's grip with her left hand, and stepped back. She pointed her pistol at Peter's face.

It's over. Peter knew it. She was going to pull the trigger. No question. He'd rolled the dice and almost pulled it off. He'd at least killed that motherfucker Sven.

If only he could get hold of Alicia. He'd teach the fucking

bitch a lesson or ten.

Alicia spun away from him, toward the back of the car. Pointing the gun at—

"*Lizzie!*"

Euphoria flooded through Peter. He wasn't dead yet after all! That fucking bitch Alicia had two guns and he had none, but she wasn't pointing either one of them at him now.

And why? Because Lizzie—*fucking Lizzie!*—was taking wide-eyed zombie steps toward Alicia and didn't seem to care that a gun was pointed at her! Just kept coming, her mouth moving as was Alicia's. Belatedly, Peter realized he couldn't hear either of them. Could only hear the deafening echo of the recent gunfire.

Jubilation erupted within him. He'd hit the long shot. Had had almost no chance at all but could now pull the rabbit out of his hat.

Peter reached into his magician's sleeve on the underside of his right elbow for the pepper spray. Oh, baby, he'd done it! He'd done it! He could already see in his mind's eye that *fucking* bitch Alicia incapacitated, unable to see because of the pepper spray, and oh, baby, what he would do to the fucking bitch then.

He flicked the cap off the palm-sized spray bottle.

The trunk hood popped up. All above and around Lizzie, the night exploded.

Did you ever care for me at all? Lizzie had to know. *You tried to sell me as a twelve-year-old whore for pedophiles. Is that how you saw me? Did you ever care for me at all?*

A bullet whizzed by Lizzie's head.

Was it me, Peter?

Lizzie racked the slide. Extended her arm. Pulled the trigger. The huge man in the ski mask went down.

Am I that unlovable? Don't say it. I know the answer.

She climbed out of the trunk. Stepped toward the rear of the passenger side. Arm with gun down at her side. A woman pointed a gun at her. Her back to the open front door, the woman said, "You're his woman! You're the woman he tried to sell!"

Was it me, Peter? It was, wasn't it?

Lizzie said it out loud. "Was it me, Peter? It was, wasn't it?"

She took another step. Two steps away from the woman. Almost at the open side door now. Looked at Peter.

"Was it me, Peter? Or was it you?"

A familiar gleam came to Peter's eyes. He reached into a sleeve at his elbow.

"Sell me to pedophiles?"

Peter pulled a small object out of his sleeve.

Lizzie extended her arm.

Aimed.

"Was it me, Peter? Or was it you?"

Peter pulled the cap off the small object. Reached his arm out to point it—

Lizzie pulled the trigger. Emptied the entire magazine. Dropped the gun.

"Peter, it was you."

ABOUT THE EDITORS

MICHAEL BRACKEN, an award-winning writer of fiction, non-fiction, and advertising copy, has received multiple awards for copywriting, two Derringer Awards for short fiction, and the Edward D. Hoch Memorial Golden Derringer Award for lifetime achievement in short mystery fiction. The author of several books and more than 1,300 short stories (including crime fiction published in *Alfred Hitchcock's Mystery Magazine, Ellery Queen's Mystery Magazine,* and *The Best American Mystery Stories*), he has edited six crime fiction anthologies and provides editorial services to book and periodical publishers.

Michael regularly speaks about writing, editing, and publishing at conferences, conventions, and corporate seminars, and has taught non-credit courses for writers at Southern Illinois University at Edwardsville. He's been a guest speaker in classrooms at various universities, including Baylor University and University of Mary Hardin-Baylor.

He received a Bachelor of Arts in Professional Writing from Baylor University and currently serves clients and publishers from his office in Hewitt, Texas.

TREY R. BARKER is the author of the Jace Salome novels, as well as the Barefield Trilogy. He also wrote *No Harder Prison, The Cancer Chronicles,* and *Hostage,* as well as hundreds of short stories spanning every genre from horror to crime. Once a journalist, Barker is now a patrol sergeant with the Bureau County Sheriff's Office in north-central Illinois.

ABOUT THE AUTHORS

Boston-based author **DAVE ZELTSERMAN**'s short fiction has won a Shamus, Derringer, and two Ellery Queen Readers awards. His crime and horror novels have been picked as best of the year by NPR, *Washington Post*, Booklist, ALA, and WBUR. His novel *Small Crimes* has been made into a Netflix film starring Nikolaj Coster-Waldau, and his *The Caretaker of Lorne Field* is currently in film development.

STACY WOODSON made her crime fiction debut in *Ellery Queen Mystery Magazine's* Department of First Stories and won the 2018 Readers Award. Since her debut, she has placed short stories in several anthologies and publications. You can visit her at StacyWoodson.com.

DAVID H. HENDRICKSON's first novel, *Cracking the Ice*, was praised by *Booklist* as "a gripping account of a courageous young man rising above evil." He has since published six additional novels, including *Offside*, which has been adopted for high school student required reading. His short fiction has appeared in *Best American Mystery Stories 2018, Ellery Queen's Mystery Magazine*, and frequently in *Heart's Kiss, Pulphouse, Fiction River,* and other anthologies. He is a multi-finalist for the Derringer Award, and his story "Death in the Serengeti" was honored with the 2018 Derringer for Best Long Story. He has released four short story collections, including *Death in the Serengeti and Other Stories: Ten Tales of Crime*. Hendrickson has published over fifteen hundred works of nonfiction, most notably his first book for writers, *How to Get Your Book into Schools and Double Your Income with Volume Sales*, and also *Travis Roy: Quadriplegia and a Life of Purpose*. He has been honored with the Joe Concannon Hockey East Media Award and the Murray Kramer Scarlet Quill Award. Visit him online at HendricksonWriter.com. Sign up for his newsletter and get a free book! Also follow him on Facebook (davewrites), Twitter (@DHWriter), and Instagram (dhwriter7).

BOOKS

On the following pages are a few
more great titles from the
Down & Out Books publishing family.

For a complete list of books and to
sign up for our newsletter,
go to DownAndOutBooks.com.

Guns + Tacos Vol. 6
Michael Bracken and Trey R. Barker, Editors

Down & Out Books
January 2022
978-1-64396-261-0

There's a taco truck in Chicago known among a certain segment of the population for its daily specials. Late at night and during the wee hours of the morning, it isn't the food selection that attracts customers, it's the illegal weapons available with the special order.

Episode 16: *Refried Beans and a Snub-Nosed .44* by Hugh Lessig; Episode 17: *Two Steak Taco Combos and a Pair of Sig Sauers* by Neil S. Plakcy; Episode 18: *A Smith & Wesson with a Side of Chorizo* by Andrew Welsh-Huggins

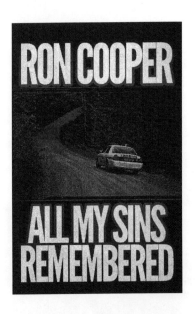

All My Sins Remembered
Ron Cooper

Down & Out Books
November 2021
978-1-64396-240-5

Deputy Sheriff Blevins Bombardi tries to solve a mysterious murder, find his estranged daughter, battle his inner demons of depression and heavy drinking and guilt for his wife's recent murder, and perhaps find the elusive Skunk Ape before a tremendous hurricane destroys north central Florida.

"Cooper is a superb writer, and a daring one too." —Steve Yarbrough, author of *The Unmade World* and *The Realm of Last Chances*

Forced Perspective
A Grant & McNulty Thriller
Colin Campbell

Down & Out Books
December 2021
978-1-64396-241-2

Jim Grant enlists Vince McNulty's help to invite criminals to audition as movie extras. The plan is almost derailed when McNulty and Grant protect a girl from an angry biker but the plan is successful. Mostly.

Except the sting is a dry run for the main person Grant wants to arrest; a crime lord movie buff in Loveland, Colorado. A sting that won't be nearly as successful.

Person Unknown
Michael Penncavage

All Due Respect, an imprint of
Down & Out Books
October 2021
978-1-64396-223-8

Life is going great for Steve Harrison. Only thirty-five years old, he's already a Senior Vice President for a major financial firm. He's admired by his co-workers, his friends, his wife—and his mistress. There's nothing he can't handle. The world, as they say, is his oyster.

And all of that is about to change…

Made in the USA
Middletown, DE
12 April 2022